NINE DEAD MEN

Ten years after his life is saved, Jason drifts into Inspiration. He believes fate has given him an opportunity to repay the debt when he hears of the leader of an outlaw gang, Adam One-ear. But his determination to meet Adam is complicated by the intervention of a sheriff who wants to kill the outlaw, a young man seeking revenge for an old injustice, and the abduction of the rancher's daughter. When Jason, the sheriff and Adam meet for the final time, nine men have already died. . .

WALTER L. BRYANT

◆

NINE DEAD MEN

Complete and Unabridged

LINFORD
Leicester

First published in Great Britain in 2012 by
Robert Hale Limited
London

First Linford Edition
published 2014
by arrangement with
Robert Hale Limited
London

A catalogue record for this book is available
from the British Library.

ISBN 978–1–4448–2064–5

Published by
F. A. Thorpe (Publishing)
Anstey, Leicestershire

Set by Words & Graphics Ltd.
Anstey, Leicestershire
Printed and bound in Great Britain by
T. J. International Ltd., Padstow, Cornwall

This book is printed on acid-free paper

To my family

Prologue

The small band of soldiers ahead of the main Union troops were faced with a bombardment of heavy artillery and musketry fire, yet still they were urged forward.

The sergeant screamed commands, his voice barely rising above the din. The officers rode among the men, encouraging, threatening, attempting to obtain order out of what seemed like chaos.

Jason Flowers, just seventeen years old and a private soldier in the Union army, was scared. He had eagerly volunteered to enlist at the commencement of the Civil War and had found it easy to lie about his age. Romantic notions about fighting had filled his mind and at first it had seemed like fun, making forays, pushing the enemy from their positions.

Soon he discovered that he was unprepared for the savagery he witnessed as he was thrown into the heat of the conflict. He hated the killing although often he had no choice but to defend himself.

The noise of the artillery and small arms and the screams of the wounded made it difficult to hear the orders of those directing the fighting. The ground was soon a morass of mud and blood.

At a brief lull in the firing he pushed on with the rest of the men, exhausted, in a daze, through the smoke and the dead and dying bodies of men and horses. They crossed a field and entered the edge of a wood where they found the enemy waiting for them.

With fixed bayonets they were urged forward and were immediately met by volleys of grapeshot and rifle balls that took many of the men before they had advanced more than a few steps. The enemy emerged from their cover and they in turn were decimated by the superior Henry rifles held by some of the Union soldiers.

Jason had little idea of the passage of time. He must have been fighting for many hours, intent on doing his duty even though many of the men and officers had demonstrated their cowardice. He fired, reloaded and fired again and again, continuing to advance while men around him dropped.

Then it was his turn to receive a musket shot in the chest that sent him spinning to the ground in a wave of agony. He fell and the battle continued without him.

He was aware that he was still alive, but when he found the strength to examine his wound he knew his end had come. He lay still and thought of his home and family as it had been before his ma died and his pa took to the bottle. Despite it all he never once questioned why he had been fighting and why he was now dying.

He was aroused by something prodding at his body and a voice speaking to him, it seemed, from a great distance.

In his confusion he was sure he had been found by his sergeant and he said a prayer of thanks as hope gave him the will to open his eyes.

He was wrong. A confederate soldier stood over him with the point of a bayonet poised at his throat. He shut his eyes and awaited the inevitable.

The next thing he knew he was lying on a bed of moss sipping warm water from a canteen. He was being supported by the soldier with an arm around his shoulder. As he drank Jason noticed a crimson stream of blood flowing from the man's face where his ear had been shot off.

'You're wounded,' he murmured unnecessarily.

The soldier grinned. 'Not half as bad as you. Difference is I can walk an' you can't. Now, this is gonna hurt a mite.' He hoisted Jason up on to his shoulders.

It was agony. Jason screamed in pain and fainted.

He later felt himself being carried,

slipping in and out of consciousness, partly aware of the clamour of shouts, curses, voices raised in anger and, above all, the confusion of people, mules and ambulances as they transported the wounded to the makeshift field hospitals.

The next time he awoke he was being tended by a young woman whom he took to be a nurse. Her dress and apron were covered with blood and there was a dead look in her eyes as though they had seen too much.

'You're lucky to be alive,' she told him as she cut away his clothing to reveal the wound beneath. He heard her gasp.

'How did I get here?' he mumbled.

'Carried,' she said. 'A young Reb. Had his ear shot off, poor boy. We patched him up, couldn't do nothing else, and he left sudden like. Now lie still.'

He did as he was told, heard a man's voice say, 'Keep him comfortable. He probably won't make it through the night.'

5

Soft hands adjusted the covers which had been placed over him. He smiled and said his prayers again before he lost consciousness once more without learning the identity of his rescuer.

1

Ten years later Jason Flowers sat easily in the saddle. He wore jeans, a check shirt with a red bandanna at the neck and a leather vest, all dust covered. On his head was a wide-brimmed Stetson which failed to cover his mop of shoulder-long, black hair. A pistol hung in a well-oiled holster at his right hip.

Under him the sorrel moved rhythmically over the uneven ground. Relaxed and at peace with the world, he felt the bullet pass close by his head at the same time as he became aware of the crack of the rifle shot. He crouched low over the back of the horse and made for a stand of pines and oak to his left. A second bullet followed him, but by then he was hidden in among the trees.

He slid quickly to the ground, sliding his Winchester from the saddle boot.

'Well done, Bess,' he said, addressing the sorrel affectionately. 'Now, I wonder what that's all about? Why would some critter try to kill me? We've come through too much to let that happen.'

He had, against all expectations, survived the War and the injury he had suffered at that time. The musket shot that had entered his chest had been deflected by one of his ribs. This and the help of the unknown Confederate soldier had saved his life. He had refused to die then and he was not intending to give up the habit now.

The years had seen big changes in him. From being an under-weight, pale youth of seventeen he had grown into a tall, powerful man, bronzed from an outdoor life, toughened by hard work. His hair had grown long, his steel-grey eyes held a wealth of experience. He had wandered West to seek his fortune and freedom from the memories of war. He had never found either.

Now, under cover of the trees, he pushed back his Stetson and screwed up his eyes as he peered through the branches, trying to get a fix on the shooter.

Rising some hundred yards away towards the west where the sun was hanging low over the nearby hills, was a stretch of rocky escarpments. He guessed it was from that direction that the shot had come and he fixed his gaze there in the hope of seeing movement that would give him something to aim at.

He remained motionless and waited, his patience being rewarded when he spotted a flash of light as the sun caught metal.

The trees stretched to his right, curving round to a draw which gave him cover until he could reach the foot of the rocks and remain out of sight of the bushwhacker.

'Stay there, Bess,' he said as he trailed the reins, crooked the rifle in his arm and began the ascent. He quickly reached the top but his effort had been in vain for there was no sign of his quarry. A search of the area revealed two spent cartridges and he put them thoughtfully into his pocket.

As he turned to make the descent he glimpsed three men, riding away at a fast pace, following the trail that ran beside the water. He shielded his eyes and watched.

'Dang it,' he muttered. 'Who the hell are you?'

He withdrew the spyglass from his belt, trained it on the fleeing figures and was rewarded with a clear image of one of the horses, a roan with a splash of white on its rump. 'Well, I'll recognize you agin when I see ya,' he muttered and folded the glass away.

With a shrug of his shoulders he continued along the trail until, two hours later, he reached the town of Inspiration and entered the main street.

Since his recovery in the war he had seen many towns as he sought his fortune, drifting from one job to another. This place was not much different from the others. The main street was wide, flanked by boardwalks fronting the brick or clapboard buildings. There were two saloons, a boarding house, a livery, undertaker's, and several businesses.

His keen grey eyes took it all in, missing little as he made his way down the rutted and dusty thoroughfare, acknowledging the occasional greeting by a brief nod. He noticed in particular the fixed and intense expression on the face of the young man, no more than seventeen, riding a grey, as they passed each other. Something about the youth was disturbing, but Jason decided it was none of his business.

He was also aware of the well-dressed man seated astride a palomino. The man was neatly dressed in a white shirt tied at the neck by a black cravat, grey pants and long, open jacket. His hair was black, sleek and shiny. His face was clean-shaven.

Jason continued along the length of the street until he found the livery. 'Treat Bess special,' he told the livery man, and silver passed between them. He gathered his belongings, hoisted them over his shoulder and went in search of some food. An hour later, refreshed by a meal of beef stew and home-made rolls, followed by cherry pie and coffee, he made his way to the nearby saloon, the Golden Apple.

He still had a few dollars left and, before they were gone, he hoped fate would provide for him as it had so often in the past.

His eyes raked along the row of horses tethered at the rail and he drew in his breath sharply when he saw the white patch he had last seen through the spyglass.

The sound of many voices and the strains of a piano reached him as he pushed through the batwings and walked casually over to the far end of the polished bar. His eyes swept around the room and took in at a glance the occupants of the saloon, hoping to identify the bushwhacker.

Everything appeared normal. The

doves were intent on plying their trade around the men who were the objects of their attention. The men at the tables were showing more interest in their hands of cards than in the women or the appearance of a stranger.

Those already at the bar gave him no more than a passing glance and continued with the important business of telling tales and drinking.

Jason liked it that way. He didn't welcome undue attention. His experiences in the war and his solitary wanderings since had given him a liking for privacy, but it had also shortened his temper and made him quick to react.

'Ya best whiskey,' he said to the barman. His voice was soft.

He took the glass and swallowed the contents quickly, then let the after-taste linger for a moment before signalling for a refill. As the barman tilted the bottle Jason grabbed his arm and twisted it, so that several fingers of whiskey spilled on the polished surface.

'I asked fer ya best,' he said quietly.

The barman grimaced. 'No need to git rough,' he grumbled. 'My mistake.' He corked the bottle, mopped up the spilled liquor and reached under the counter.

Jason's reaction was swift. He leaned forward and grasped the barman by the collar. 'What else've ya got hid under there?'

'Only a bottle, mister. Only a bottle. You're a mite nervous, ain't ya? What did ya reckon? A shotgun mebbe?'

Now heads were being turned in Jason's direction. He met their gaze without blinking. 'Jus' bein' cautious,' he said. Reaching into his pocket he pulled out a handful of silver and placed it on the counter. 'How many glasses'll that buy me?'

The barman arched his eyebrows and hesitated for a moment, scooped up the money and grinned. 'I'll let ya know when you've had enough,' He refilled the glass and Jason left it standing.

One of the doves, probably now past

her best but striving to appear young, with a low-cut silken dress tight across her bosom, sidled up to him. He noticed the tiredness in her eyes and the lines around her mouth as she held on to his arm and smiled up at him.

'They call me Marl. What's yer name, mister?' she asked in a voice that Jason thought might once have been sweet but had now been soured by smoke and whiskey.

Jason returned her smile. 'Like to git to know you. Really would,' he said. 'Mebbe later. But fer now all the cash I've got's tied up in that bottle.' He gestured towards the bar. 'You're welcome to a glass outa that.' He sent a questioning look across the counter and was encouraged by a nod.

'Yer good fer a few more,' the barman said.

The woman flashed her teeth. 'Just one, then.' She drained the glass swiftly. 'Thanks. Perhaps another time?'

'Yep. Another time.'

'You gonna be in town fer long?'

Jason hesitated. 'All depends,' he said.

'I'm here permanent.'

'Well, Marl, I'll be sure to look you up.'

She shrugged. As she made her way back to try her luck on someone else Jason was aware that he was now the object of some curiosity and also that Marl was the butt of some coarse jokes by the men at the bar. He watched her with some sympathy. Although he couldn't clearly hear what the men were saying it was obvious that some of the jokes were also coming his way.

He withdrew his Colt from its holster and laid it on the counter next to the whiskey glass.

'Take care o' that,' he said to the barman and then walked casually over to the group of men. He laid his hand on the shoulder of her main tormentor, a man dressed in blue shirt and jeans. A grey moustache swept down each side of his mouth, the rest of his face was tanned by an outdoor life. He was a large man and Jason judged him to be both fit and strong, his senses perhaps a little dulled just now by an excess of drink. Jason recalled that Marl had called him Duke.

'If you've got things to say about me say 'em to my face,' Jason said quietly.

The man turned quickly and unexpectedly swung a wild punch. Jason's hand shot out and held his forearm in a grip of steel. Jason twisted and pushed the arm up behind the man's back.

'No need fer that,' Jason grated. 'I'm only tryin' to be helpful.' He released his hold.

Duke straightened. 'Who the hell're you?' His eyes dropped to Jason's empty holster. 'Where's yer gun? Ya had one when you came in.'

'Kinda gets in the way of friendly discussion, don't ya think?'

'This ain't a discussion,' Duke grated. 'And it certainly ain't friendly.' He looked at his companion, a smaller, wiry man, for support. 'What d'ya think, Zeb?'

Zeb grinned, his eyes, fired by liquor,

glinting with the excitement of a fight. 'Yep. Don't seem friendly to me.'

'Have it your way,' Jason said, refusing to back down. 'I'm gonna ask one question and we'll call it quits. Who's ridin' the chestnut out by the hitch rail? One with the white.'

The reaction was sudden. Duke's face turned red and his eyes held anger. 'Askin' questions like that can get a man into trouble,' he growled. 'What fer d'ya wanna know?'

Jason slid the bullet casings from his pocket and held them out in the palm of his hand. 'Because,' he began slowly, 'whosoever owns that horse also owns these an' I'll be mighty pleased to meet him.'

Duke hesitated and his face broke into a wicked smirk. 'So now you've met him. I wunnered if I'd meet the *hombre* trespassing on Carter Brown property.'

'Trail was clear enough,' Jason said.

'You were still trespassing,' the man repeated.

18

'I was sort of hopin' this might've bin a friendly place. If you reckoned I was trespassing you could've rode up and told me so 'stead of tryin' to kill me.'

'Mister,' Duke said with an edge to his voice, 'if I'd tried to put a slug in you back there you'd be eatin' dirt right now. You got the message an' you're still standin'. But I'm willin' to have another go, if you're so minded. An' this time I might even hit the target.'

This brought a grunt of mirth from his companion.

'If yer lookin' fer trouble you've found it,' Duke continued.

This was not what Jason was looking for. He wanted answers, not gun play.

'After I've put lead in you,' he reasoned, 'you'll not be able to tell me what I wanna know. An' if you lay a slug in me I'll never git to know the answer to my question. So, how's about you an' me sharing the rest of that bottle over there and talkin' to each other like men?'

'I'm done talking,' Duke growled, the

whiskey forming the words for him. 'Pick up yer gun. I'll be outside waitin' for ya.' He turned on his heel and left unsteadily through the batwings, leaving Jason with nowhere to go but to follow.

He walked slowly over to the bar, picked up his Colt, checked it and eased it into its holster. He eyed his drink but hoped he would be able to have it later. He had no idea how fast or accurate his opponent would be or how liquor might affect his aim. He knew that his own draw was little more than average.

Spectators from the saloon and the street gathered but swiftly retreated when they realized there was to be shooting.

They faced each other, twenty paces apart in the dust of the street, with daylight fading and the kerosene lamps not yet making much impression. Jason had no wish to kill another man but also had no desire to be killed.

He decided to take a chance. With his

hand well away from his holster he walked forward, maintaining eye contact and closing the gap between Duke and himself until the two men were face to face with inches between them.

'I've no wish to see you die,' he hissed. 'And I'm not ready to meet my Maker just yet.'

His hand shot forward and, with a swift movement that confused the big man, swept Duke's gun from its holster. At the same time he removed his own and threw both weapons up on to the boardwalk.

For one brief moment Duke didn't move, surprised at such an unexpected turn of events. Then, 'Goddamn it!' he roared. He drew back his lips in an ugly snarl and a fleck of spittle appeared at the corner of his mouth. 'You'll be pickin' yer teeth outa the dust fer that.'

His attack was more disciplined this time. A fist of iron caught Jason on the side of the head and he rocked backwards, senses swimming. He felt as if he'd been hit with a lump of rock.

Duke followed up quickly and another controlled swing sent him spinning on to his back. From the corner of his eye Jason saw the boot coming. He rolled, grabbed and twisted the heavy foot viciously, gratified to hear the grunt of pain from his attacker.

This had less effect than he might have expected. Duke stumbled backwards, wrenched his foot free and came forward again. But Jason was up and ready and threw more punches that stopped Duke in his tracks.

The man stumbled and Jason took the opportunity to send a succession of hard and accurate punches that connected with Duke's face and head. The man's eyes glazed and a well-aimed uppercut sat him in the dust.

Duke shook his head and a deep growl came up from his chest as he heaved himself to his feet. He was far from finished.

Blood was pouring from both men where fists had landed and Jason wondered if he had taken on too much as Duke rained more blows on him. Most of them were parried easily but some made it through Jason's guard and hurt.

While Jason was recovering from a punch that rattled his ribcage Duke scrambled to gather up his gun from the sidewalk.

'This is how we deal with polecats like you.' He raised the barrel and thumbed back the hammer.

2

How the confrontation would have ended Jason was not to find out. Oblivion perhaps. But before that could happen Zeb had grabbed Duke's gun hand at the same time as an angry shout broke the tension. Duke's finger was only a twitch away from sending hot lead into Jason's chest and at such a short distance the outcome would have been inevitable. As it was the bullet sped harmlessly into the air.

'Stop! That's enough!'

The voice held authority. Jason turned and recognized the man as the one he had seen earlier, handsome, with a mouth that might smile easily, although at that moment it was set in a determined straight line. His piercing blue eyes glared down at Jason's aggressor. His clothes and bearing showed him to be someone of substance.

It was not obvious to Jason that the man was physically handicapped until he dismounted, Zeb stepping forward to lift him from the saddle. He stood with the aid of a stick.

But it was the young woman, leading a pinto, who drew Jason's attention. He judged she was in her early twenties, attractive in a boyish way, dressed in jeans and white shirt, with a rounded face and black hair that flowed down to her shoulders. Father and daughter, he surmised, for she had her pa's deep-blue eyes which were now looking with some distaste at Jason's unkempt appearance. He was suddenly aware of the dust and grime in his clothes and hair.

Her pa was angry. 'Duke, I don't pay you to shoot strangers. What kind of impression d'you think that gives about this town?'

'Sorry, boss,' Duke said, although he didn't sound it. 'But we caught him trespassing.'

'Well, he's not trespassing now, is

he?' There was steel in his gaze.

'No, boss.'

'Right, now we've cleared that up I suggest you go inside and continue with whatever you were doing. I'd like to chat with this gentleman here.' He turned to Jason. 'I'm Carter Brown, owner of the CB ranch. I'm not partial to my men behaving in this way.'

With a final glare in Jason's direction that told him this matter wasn't finished, Duke thrust himself through the batwings, reholstering his gun on the way. Zeb remained and Carter Brown turned his anger on him.

'Why'd you let this happen?'

'You know what Duke's like,' Zeb said. 'An' I stopped him, din't I?'

Carter Brown glared. 'Just as well or you'd both be looking for another job.' To Jason he said, 'Give me a moment, I need to talk to the men.' He shuffled through the batwings, followed by Zeb, leaving Jason alone with the girl.

He picked up his own gun, examined it and slipped it into its holster.

Although he was tongue-tied for a moment by the girl's presence, she showed no signs of embarrassment.

'Pa doesn't like his men making gun play in the street,' she said. 'Duke would've killed you, you know. I'm amazed Zeb didn't let him. Both men are dangerous.' The directness of her statement took him by surprise. 'You were lucky.'

'Mebbe,' he admitted. 'But then it could've bin him laying in the dust an' I wouldn't've liked that either. I'm sorta glad you turned up.' He rubbed his bruised knuckles ruefully.

'Don't get the idea that Zeb stopped the fight on your account,' she said. 'I'll guess he saw Pa and knew the rules that Pa has set for his men. Zeb's a good ramrod, whatever else he may be, an' you may be a gunslinger for all he knew. Are you?'

'I'm not,' Jason told her. 'I came in peaceful an' I want it to stay that way.'

Her eyes flashed. 'Pa wouldn't've batted an eyelid if you'd bin laid out in the dirt. Me neither,' she added, although her smile softened what she was saying. 'Just a word of warning. Watch your back and don't start anything you can't finish.'

Before Jason could ask her what she meant her pa came out of the saloon. 'Grace, you go on home. I'll join you shortly after I've talked to our friend here.'

Grace nodded. 'OK, Pa.' She flashed a brief smile in Jason's direction, swung herself up easily on her horse and rode away.

Jason watched her depart.

'You going to stand there all day?' Carter Brown asked, a hint of amusement playing round the corners of his mouth.

Jason turned and mounted the three steps to the board-walk. The rancher studied him with penetrating blue eyes. 'Have you got a name?'

'Jason. Jason Flowers.'

'Passing through or what?'

'Not sure yet. Depends on whether I like this town.'

'And whether the town likes you,' Carter Brown said. 'Not a good start, I'd say, gettin' into a fight with one of my hands.'

'Yeah, well, weren't my intent. They bushwhacked me.'

The rancher looked at him sharply. 'I guess they didn't hurt you any.'

'I don't take to bein' shot at.'

Carter Brown pointed to the pistol that Jason had slipped back into its holster. 'You any good with that?'

'Good as the next man,' Jason admitted. 'Some would say better.'

'Are they right?'

'There've bin a few who've found out.' It was true but he preferred not to boast about it.

There was silence between them and Jason felt himself being assessed.

'I might have a proposition to put to you,' Carter Brown continued.

Jason shook his head. He'd met situations similar to this before. 'You've made a mistake. I'm not a hired gun. If that's what you're wantin' I'm sure there's plenty to be had at the right price.'

'Hear me out,' the rancher rapped. 'I don't want a hired gun. I can get as many of them as I want. I'm offering you a job.' His gaze took in Jason's soiled clothes and unkempt appearance. 'Seems to me you could do with one.'

'I'm not denyin' it.'

The older man didn't smile. 'If I guess right, you'll be well used to working with cows and horses.'

'Yep, but my gun's not fer hire.'

This time Jason was rewarded with a scowl that furrowed the rancher's brow.

'I've answered that already. Mebbe I've made a mistake.' He hesitated, his eyes unreadable, before he continued. 'Zeb's my foreman as well as my . . . ' He left the sentence unfinished, then went on, 'He tells me we ought to take you on. The ranch happens to be short-handed.'

Jason raised his eyebrows in disbelief. After what had just happened this was an unexpected turn of events. 'I kin turn my hand to most things,' he said.

'You'll be taking orders from Zeb. You OK with that?'

'I kin take orders from anyone s'long as they're fair.'

'You running from the law?'

Jason shook his head. 'Nope. Always thought it best to stay on the right side.'

Carter Brown seemed satisfied. 'Good. I'm gonna make some cash available to you in the bank. You can pay me back sometime if you're so minded. Mention my name to the manager.' He smiled. 'I guess you ain't got much to call your own just now.'

Jason grinned in return. All he had was what he carried around with him and a few dollar bills tucked neatly into his boot for emergencies. 'You could say that.'

'Right.' The rancher signified that the meeting was at an end. 'Now, help me on my horse. I'll be at the ranch tomorrow. Can I expect you?'

Jason nodded. 'Yep, I'll be there.'

'And,' the rancher added, 'get your-self a bath and a good night's sleep at Rosie's hotel. Tell her I sent you.' He turned the palomino and urged it forward.

Jason gazed after him, wondering what he had let himself in for. Naturally, the fact that he would meet the lovely Grace again had nothing to do with his decision.

Remembering the drink waiting for him at the bar he pushed open the batwings and entered the saloon. As soon as he did so he knew there was trouble waiting as he saw that Zeb and Duke had occupied his place at the counter. Moreover, Zeb was now holding Jason's glass of whiskey.

Neither man moved as Jason approached.

'Good liquor,' Zeb said, holding the glass up to the light.

Jason moved close. 'Already spoken fer,' he grated.

'Yeah, well, I'll drink to that.'

Jason reached out and laid his hand gently on Zeb's forearm. He leaned forward and spoke into Zeb's ear. 'Suit yerself, but if you reckon to drink that without bein' invited I'll be obliged to break yer fingers. And then,' he added, 'I'll have to break yer arm.'

The two men held each other's gaze. Zeb was the first to look away as he replaced the glass on the bar. 'No sense in arguing jest now,' he said, with a meaningful glance at Duke. 'But this ain't the end.'

Keeping a wary eye on both men, Jason picked up the glass, tipped the contents down his throat, turned and walked out without a backward glance. It had been an eventful day, he thought, as he made his way to Rosie's place. He might have stored up trouble for himself but he walked with a light step, prepared for anything that might come his way.

* * *

Although he had plenty to occupy his mind he slept well and next morning

33

awoke to the smell of cooking bacon. As soon as the bank opened he would find out what the day held in store for him. He was in no hurry as he strolled down the main street.

The bank sat in the centre of the town, opposite the sheriff's office. A grey was tethered outside. The building was not large but solidly brick-built and Jason walked up the steps and through the heavy open door.

He paused inside and studied the interior. There were two tellers' windows but only one was occupied, where a businessman was in conversation with a young clerk behind the metal grille.

The only other person in the room was a slight young man with his back to Jason, peering out of the small barred window. Something odd about the way he was standing caused Jason to look more closely. But it wasn't until he turned his head that Jason recognized him as the young man who had passed him in the street the evening before.

He still wore the strained expression

Jason had previously noticed with the eyes fixed and the mouth set as if he had focused his mind on a particular course of action. He made no move towards the teller's window. Something outside was keeping his attention.

Jason was curious and glanced back across the street where the sheriff was leaning against a wooden post enjoying the morning sun and drawing heavily on his cigar. A tin star was pinned to his vest.

It was not until the sheriff sauntered away up the street that the young man made his move, pulling his bandanna up over his face, drawing his gun from its holster and taking a step forward. A gunny sack was visible under his jacket.

Jason guessed his intentions immediately. By this time there were no other customers in the bank. Without thinking he leaped into the young man's path, grabbed his gun arm and pushed him back against the wall. The bandanna slipped. His face looked more boyish than before despite the wild look in his eyes.

'What the hell're you aimin' to do with that?' Jason demanded, trying to keep his voice low.

'Get outa my way!' the young man hissed and struggled to free himself from Jason's iron grip. His thumb pulled back on the hammer.

Jason attempted to wrest the weapon from his grasp but, with the gun already cocked and a finger curled round the trigger, it was inevitable that the Colt fired. A slug sped across the room and embedded itself in the opposite wall. The noise of the shot was magnified in the confined place.

'Dammit to hell,' the youth grated. 'Look what you've done now. Everybody will've heard that shot.'

Jason managed to take the gun from him. 'What I've done? I've stopped you making a goddamnn fool of yerself. D'ya think you could've robbed the bank with a pistol and a gunny sack? All by yerself?'

The sound of the shot had several results.

The clerk gasped and sped away from his post, leaving Jason and the boy alone.

The manager of the bank rushed out and then retreated when he saw what he thought were two armed men.

A voice shouted from the street, 'This is the sheriff. Show yerselves, you varmints. You're surrounded. You can't get away. Throw out yer weapons or we're comin' in to get ya.'

3

'Best do as he says,' Jason said. Then he called, 'OK Sheriff. We're comin' out.'

He threw out the two pistols and guided the young man through the doorway, both with their hands held high.

There was a grin as wide as a barn door on the sheriff's face. 'Well, well, what have we here? Keep yer hands up high.' He held a shotgun steady and pointed at the two bank robbers.

Jason wasn't about to argue and the youngster was silent when he saw the reception waiting for him. A crowd had soon gathered and there wasn't a friendly face to be seen.

'No foolish moves,' Jason told his companion. 'One twitch of that trigger finger an' we're both peppered with buckshot.'

The sheriff gestured towards his

office and followed them closely, never letting his attention wander. Once inside the building he unhooked a bunch of keys from the wall, urged his captives towards the cells.

'In!' he ordered the younger man and locked the cell door. 'You,' he said, addressing Jason. 'We're gonna have us a little talk. Saddle bums like you think they can come into my town an' cause trouble. Well, I'm gonna teach you what trouble really is.'

Without warning he jabbed the barrel of the shotgun into Jason's back with such force that it sent him staggering forward on to his knees.

'What in tarnation did ya do that fer?' Jason roared. 'I ain't no outlaw. I saved your town from bein' robbed.' He rose to his feet and glared at the sheriff.

The lawman pointed to the wooden chair in front of the large desk. 'Sit down an' shut up till I tell you to speak.' He leaned back in his own chair with a growl of satisfaction, keeping his gun resting on the polished surface of the open-fronted desk and pointing in Jason's direction.

Jason studied him. The man was overweight, probably in his fifties, with a lined, clean-shaven face. Grey eyes looked out upon the world with an expression of weary mistrust. His pale shirt showed signs of sweat and, although the atmosphere in the office was hot, he kept his broad-brimmed hat firmly on his head.

The desk and old leather chair took up about half the office. The other half contained a pot-bellied stove on which a tin jug of coffee was steaming, the chair in which Jason was sitting, some files on a shelf, a rack of guns, securely chained, and little else. A board held some notices and Wanted posters, all haphazardly pinned together.

One poster in particular caught his attention, offering $5,000 reward, dead or alive, for the outlaw, Adam Redford, also known as Adam One-ear, wanted for murder and robbery.

'That's a heap o'money,' Jason

observed and rose from his chair to have a closer look. He pulled the poster from the wall and laid it on the desk to get a better sight of it.

'Looks sorta like you, don't he,' the lawman grated. 'Now siddown! I won't tell you agin.'

Jason obliged.

The sheriff applied a match to a large cigar. 'I'm Kelly Quintock an' I'm the sheriff here, as you might've guessed, an' I uphold law and order hereabouts. So I don't take kindly to bank robbers. Tell me what you were plannin' in the bank an' how you thought you'd get away.' Smoke drifted up.

Jason sat, gazing into the lawman's eyes trying to gauge exactly what lay there. But before answering the sheriff's question he had one of his own. He pointed to the poster. 'Who is he?'

'No concern o' yours.' The sheriff sent a stream of tobacco juice into the spittoon.

'It's only I might've known him,' Jason said. The picture on the dodger

41

was unclear and the memory of his rescuer had faded over the years.

'It's like the poster says, he's wanted fer robbery an' murder. So the story goes he got his ear shot off fightin' fer the Rebs. I'm aimin' to shoot the other one off afore long an' then put a slug between the two. He's dangerous. Best left to the law. If you're in cahoots with that varmint then you're in real trouble. Now,' he said, losing patience, 'you can answer my questions.'

Jason told him everything that had happened. He saw doubt in the sheriff's face but this softened at the mention of Carter Brown's offer.

'You're gonna work fer the CB ranch?'

'Dunno yet but that's the general idea. Long as you don't lock me up in one of ya cells.'

The sheriff thought for a moment. 'Mebbe yer tellin' me the truth an' mebbe not. Anyways I'm a busy man an' I've a notion to believe you.' He reached a sudden decision, picked up the keys and threw them to Jason. 'Go get the boy and bring the keys back here.'

When the young man entered the office it was clear that his aggression had returned. His face held an embittered hardness.

'Siddown on that chair,' Kelly Quintock ordered. 'You're gonna make a statement and I'm gonna write it down.' He thumbed through the pages of a thick ledger, found a pencil that would write, then he looked up at Jason. 'You still here? I've told ya, I'm not gonna lock you up but I'm warnin' ya to keep the peace or I'll jump on ya.'

Jason hesitated. 'I'd rather like to hear what our young friend has to say if you don't mind, Sheriff. I'm sorta involved.'

'Suit yerself.' The sheriff turned his attention towards the youngster. 'Let's start with yer name.'

The youth looked everywhere but at the sheriff. Suddenly he, too, noticed the law dodger. He jabbed his finger on it. 'You'll never catch him,' he shouted. 'Never. He's too smart fer all of ya.'

The sheriff rose, walked around the desk and viciously back-handed the young man across his face. Blood spurted from his nose.

'No need fer that,' Jason hissed.

The sheriff ignored him and resumed his seat. He leaned back. 'What's yer name, kid?' he growled. 'I'll not be askin' you agin.'

'Billy. Billy Manning.' The boy's voice was harsh with emotion. 'And I'm not a kid.'

'Oh, so you're a man. How old are ya?'

'Seventeen. You may cotton on to who I am. Do ya?'

'Don't reckon as I do.'

'Nigh on eight years ago. You were still sheriff here when we was driven out of our farm. You did nothin' fer us then. You still in the pocket of Carter Brown?'

Jason saw a flash of recognition in the sheriff's eyes.

The lawman sneered. 'Is that what this is all about, you robbin' the bank an' all? You aimin' to become an outlaw like that feller?' He pointed to the poster. 'If you are you'll not live long enough to see yer next birthday.'

'He's twice the man you are,' Billy said.

'We'll see about that!'

The big man moved around the desk at speed and this time he laid into the boy with such vigour that the chair tipped over backwards, spilling him to the floor.

Jason leaped forward and, grabbing the sheriff by the shoulders, heaved him across the room. 'He's just a boy! He don't deserve that sorta treatment.' He held out his hand to help Billy up.

The sheriff went red in the face and, as he recovered his balance, his hand dropped to his Colt.

'Seems to me,' he spat, 'that both of you seem to be acquainted with that *hombre*. Perhaps you'd like to let me in on the secret.' He looked expectantly at both of them. 'You either tell me now or I lock the two of you up until you do.'

Billy dabbed at the blood now flowing freely from his lip. 'Yeah, I was goin' to rob the bank. I wish I had. I reckon as I'm owed. Carter Brown, the town and you took it all away when you drove us out.'

'What's that gotta do with Adam One-ear?'

'I met him out in the hills. I'd bin hurt. He picked me up. He promised to help me get justice but he said as I had to prove myself first. Robbin' the bank seemed the easiest way.' He turned to Jason. 'An' if it hadn't bin fer you I'd've done it.'

Jason shrugged. 'Mebbe. Mebbe not. Likely you'd've shot someone an' then had a rope round yer neck.' He'd been watching the sheriff when the outlaw was mentioned. 'You aimin' to catch him, Sheriff?'

'Who?'

He pointed to the poster. 'Him.'

46

'What's it to you?'

'Just like to be part of your posse if you've a mind to go chasin' after him.'

'I don't cotton to bounty hunters.'

'It ain't that,' Jason said, 'but five thousand dollars could be a sizeable incentive.' He didn't miss the glint of greed in the sheriff's eyes and wondered if the lawman had set his mind on claiming the reward.

He went on to tell the sheriff an abbreviated story of how he'd met a Confederate soldier with one ear and was interested to see if he was the same man. 'Wouldn't mind meetin' up with him again. I've a debt to pay.'

'A goddamnn Reb! Right. That about wraps it up.' Quintock yanked Billy to his feet. 'You, back in the cells.'

'But I ain't done nothing wrong,' the boy protested. 'You got no right to lock me up.' He threw up his arms to protect himself from the expected blow.

He was propelled by the sheriff's strong right arm through the door connecting the office to the cells. 'I got every right. Intention to rob. Firing yer gun in a bank. Frightening yer fellow citizens. Resistin' an officer of the law.

'I gotta protect the citizens of this town. I'm gonna put you where you belong till I've made up my mind what to do with you.'

With a final glance at the poster Jason got up to leave. 'Tell yer prisoner I'll take his horse to the livery,' he said.

The sheriff grunted and licked his pencil, ready to fill in his report, but at that moment the door of the office was thrust open. The man who burst in was small and neatly dressed in a dark-grey suit and polished shoes. His hair was slicked back and shiny as though it had been polished.

'Sheriff, you gotta do something about it!'

4

Kelly Quintock looked up, annoyed at the sudden interruption.

'What's the problem, Ethan? Town council got more complaints? Won't it wait? I'm kinda busy.'

The problem obviously wouldn't wait and, ignoring the presence of Jason, Ethan launched straight in. 'He's done it again. The stage was held up an hour ago. Up by Pilgrim's Pass. It's the Redford gang again! An' they get away with it every time. Yeah, the town council's not happy. I'm not happy. What're you gonna do about it?'

'Anyone killed?'

'One passenger injured, two dead. But the bank's gold's bin taken.'

Jason kept silent, waiting for more, but the sheriff looked at him in some surprise. 'You still here? Thought I told ya to get out.'

'Just going, Sheriff. If I could have my Colt back I won't get unner your hide no more.'

Without a word the sheriff reached into the desk drawer and removed Jason's gun. He held it as if deciding what to do with it.

'I've a mind to keep it, but then agin I guess I've no cause. But I'm tellin' ya, any more trouble outa you an' you'll be keeping him company.' He jerked his thumb in the direction of the cells, then handed the Colt reluctantly to its owner. 'Got my drift?'

Jason nodded and reholstered his weapon. 'I'll be as good as gold. You'll have no problem with me. I came here peaceful and that's how I want it to stay.'

He acknowledged Ethan and went slowly to the door. As he closed it behind him he heard the name of Adam One-ear and guessed the outlaw and his gang had been active in the area for some time. Now the sheriff was being urged to take some action against him.

Jason reasoned that that would mean a posse, but he had to discover the truth about the outlaw for himself before that happened. Perhaps young Billy Manning was the one who could help him, but the youth was locked in a cell and was going nowhere.

He looked down at himself and realized that he was still dressed in his dirty travel clothes and that there was money waiting for him in the bank. Perhaps now was the time to make use of that and to start looking less like a saddle bum. But first there was something he had to do.

Further down the street a hand-painted sign was fixed to the wall outside the offices of the local paper, aptly named the *Inspiration Clarion*. Time, he thought, to find out all he could about his new employer and anything else that might be of interest.

He peered through the dusty window and could just make out the figure of a man labouring over a printing press. He wore an overall over an open necked shirt with the sleeves rolled up.

The door opened easily but the rattle of the machinery masked the sound of his entrance. Jason watched the man for a minute or so, noticing the stooped shoulders and the greying hair. He waited for the noise to stop.

The room was filled with benches, stacks of paper, banks of type and, towards the back, piles of newspapers. Despite its cluttered appearance it gave the impression of being clean and orderly.

The man looked up but continued what he was doing. 'Didn't see you come in. What kin I do for ya?' he shouted and wiped his hands on a clean rag. Piercing blue eyes topped by thick eyebrows that moved up and down as he spoke peered out from a thin face.

'Need some information,' Jason said. 'Like to have a look at some back pages.'

'Have you got a name?'

'Yeah, Jason. Jason Flowers. I've just drifted into town.'

'So I heard,' the grey-haird man grinned. 'Brung trouble with you, too. Most folk appreciate how you stood up to those cowhands from the CB. Not many left alive who can boast of that.'

'News gets around fast here, I guess.'

'This is a newspaper if you hadn't noticed. Don't concern yerself. I kin cause trouble sometimes. I get it, too. Name's Hal Skandy. I'm the proprietor, editor, newshound, printer, salesman, general dogsbody. Anything particular ya lookin fer?'

'Local rancher, Carter Brown. I'm gonna work for him. An' the sheriff. I'd like to know a little more about him, too.'

'Yeah, you've had a run-in with our Kelly Quintock. Well, help yerself.' Skandy pointed to the piles of old papers. 'But if you'd jest give me a hand here I kin probably tell you all you want to know. I warn ya now, you'll need to be on yer guard out at the CB ranch.

'Our big rancher's not all he appears to be. An' if you've made an enemy of

Zeb Stover an' his sidekick, Duke, you'd best be doubly careful. They're unpredictable. Vicious might be a better description. Especially Zeb, who usually holds back an' gets Duke to do his dirty work.'

This information confirmed Jason's own first impression of Carter Brown and his foreman. 'Much obliged by the warning. If Zeb's such a wild stallion why does Carter Brown keep him on?'

Hal stopped printing but continued to shout until he realized he had no need to. 'Ah, of course, you wouldn't know by lookin' at them. Zeb is the rancher's brother. Well, half brother. Same ma but different pa. It was Carter Brown's pa who owned and developed the ranch and he passed it on to his son, Carter, when he found out that Zeb wasn't his. But later Carter's ma made a condition that Zeb was to be retained as foreman. Zeb's bin resentful ever since.'

'And,' Jason said, trying not to sound too interested, 'what about the girl, his daughter? Where does she fit in?'

'Ah, yes, the lovely Grace. Much admired by all the hot-blooded men in this town and outside o' it. Bit of a wildcat. Many a young buck has tried to tame her an' failed. If she takes to you she'll lead you on. If not she can give you hell.'

'I've no interest in her,' Jason admitted, and wondered whether that was true.

Hal stared at him for a moment. 'You may be the only male who hasn't. She's another reason why Zeb's bitter. She's first in line to inherit the ranch from her pa, Carter Brown.'

Jason digested this information. 'Sounds sorta interesting.'

'Yeah. Best if you kept out of it.' Hal started working on slanted trays of lead type. 'You might as well make yerself useful.'

While they worked, feeding the press, collating, stacking and bundling the finished newspapers and clearing up, Hal regaled Jason with further stories of the rancher and the man wearing the sheriff's badge.

Carter Brown had been building up his stock and expanding his land for ten years and in that time he'd made many enemies on account of his ambition and his methods. He was not a man to cross and very few people had the courage to do so. The town owed its prosperity to him.

'He had an accident some years back. Thrown from his horse and both his legs were crushed. Damage to his innards, too. Killing him slowly. Couldn't walk fer long enough but kin get about now with a stick an' some help. Made him sorta tetchy.'

'Yeah,' Jason acknowledged as he applied ink to the roller, 'S'pose it'd affect a man that way. What about the sheriff?'

The sheriff had been in post a little longer. 'When he accepted the position,' Hal said, 'he was full of good intentions and in most folk's opinion, did a good job. He's gettin' old now and has lost some of his enthusiasm. Now, I've gotta paper to get out.'

Jason took the hint and thanked his new friend for the information. 'You'll probably be seeing more of me,' he said.

'Hope so,' Hal said. 'Might be a story in you. News is a mite thin at the moment. Might even be a job here fer you if you're so minded.'

Jason left and went to the bank to withdraw his money. He expected problems but there weren't any, although he was aware of the cautious looks given to him by the teller when he was recognized. The amount he was allowed to withdraw was more than enough to fit himself out with new clothes; jeans, shirt and vest.

He found he could even replace his boots, which were showing serious signs of wear, but he retained his own hat, which had moulded itself comfortably to his head.

It was now past noon and, after a quick meal, he set off for the CB ranch.

The sun was warm and he felt relaxed and pleased with the way events were turning out. The only problem might be in settling his differences with the foreman.

He had travelled for half an hour and was now on Carter Brown land. But he was an employee and he was confident he could continue without the danger of being challenged or shot at.

In that he was wrong.

He had only just turned off the main trail at the sign for the CB ranch when, as he passed a clump of oaks and pines, a rider emerged from the shadows. He recognized Zeb immediately and also didn't miss the Winchester held firmly in the man's hands, pointing straight at his chest. He heard another horse come up behind him.

'Well, well,' Zeb growled. 'Thought we told ya to keep offa this territory.'

So much for settling differences, Jason thought. Aloud, he said. 'What's the artillery fer? I've no fight with you. I'm on my way to see Carter Brown.'

'The hell you are. There's some unfinished business we have to settle first an' I think that after that you won't be goin' nowhere.'

Jason held his gaze, seeing in the hostile stare no promise of a peaceful end to this meeting. He watched for the gun to waver, when he might have had a chance to draw his own weapon, but a sharp prod in the back caused him to think again.

Duke's voice behind him said, 'Take out yer gun. Real slow. Two fingers, left hand and throw it to the side.'

'You're makin' a mistake,' Jason said but did as he was told.

'Now git offa ya horse.'

Jason slid to the ground and waited, with Zeb's rifle still sighted on his chest.

'Kneel down!'

Because he didn't comply immediately a vicious blow across the back of his legs sent him to his knees.

'Goddamn it!' he blazed. 'What fer did you wanna do that?'

Zeb grinned. 'That's just a taste of what's to come.' He had put the rifle aside and was covering Jason with his Colt. He signalled to Duke. 'I'll cover him. You're gonna hogtie this varmint. If he makes a move I'll put a slug in him.'

'Why're ya doin' this?' Jason grated as he felt the anger well up inside him. 'There's no call fer us to fight. I'm gonna work fer the CB ranch.'

Zeb laughed loudly, the less than mirthful sound echoing off the trees. 'Who said nothin' about fighting? You're in no position to fight. And, unless you're missin' the point, you're not gonna work for no one. Fact is, I doubt you're gonna be able to work ever agin after we've finished with you.'

He strode forward and aimed a kick at Jason's ribs.

5

'Goddamn it!' Jason grunted. 'That hurt.' He realized with a shock how dangerous his situation was. If these men were allowed to hogtie him, weaponless, away from any possible help, he was in deep trouble and in danger of losing his life.

But he wasn't quite helpless.

Zeb drew back his foot to deliver another kick as Duke came up behind him ready to secure his arms.

Jason rolled with the savage kick and, as he sagged and grunted with pain, his right hand slipped back to his boot and withdrew the slim-bladed stiletto knife he carried there. He saw a third kick coming. This time he didn't let it land. Instead he sprang to his feet, hurled himself at Zeb, slipped behind him and held the blade at his throat. With his other hand he snatched the gun.

'Either of you move,' he snarled, 'and the ranch'll be looking fer a new foreman.'

Duke's Colt came up.

'Careful, Duke,' Zeb yelled. 'This blade's sharp.'

Duke didn't pause. 'He's not gonna use it,' he snarled, and his gun spat lead.

But Jason had seen the danger and had swiftly covered himself with Zeb's body.

'You shot me!' Zeb screamed as the slug, meant for Jason, hit him in the shoulder.

Duke cocked his gun a second time with the clear intention of firing again in spite of the danger to his partner.

'Git outa the way,' he screamed. He was so obviously out of control that Jason had no choice. Zeb was beginning to sag and he was finding it difficult to support him and to continue to use him as a shield.

Jason fired. He hoped merely to disable Duke long enough to wrestle the gun from him, but Zeb struggled, altering his aim, and the slug entered Duke's hip.

The gun spun from Duke's hand as he staggered back with a yelp of pain.

'Doggone it,' Jason muttered. He released Zeb, walked over to Duke and kicked the Colt out of the way. He gazed wearily at the two injured men. 'So much for a peaceful life. Now I got two wounded and angry *hombres* to deal with.'

Although both men needed medical attention Zeb was the less badly injured and Jason instructed him to deal with Duke's wound as best he could. His priority now was to get both men mounted and back to Inspiration and the doc before Duke lost too much blood.

'Goddamn it!' he said again. 'I didn't want this.'

He gathered all weapons together safely out of reach from Zeb and Duke, then tied rope to the cantles of their mounts. He inspected the arsenal he had collected and gave a wry smile.

'Dammit. I could fight off a full-scale Injun attack with these.' He stuffed them into his saddle-bags.

He was deciding on his next move when he heard a buggy approaching from the direction of the ranch. The tension left his face when the noise was accompanied by the unexpected sound of a guitar and a man singing. The reassuring mixture seemed to rule out further hostility and Jason backed up, keeping the two men covered, until he could make out who the newcomers were.

With some relief he immediately recognized the rancher's daughter holding the reins.

'Ho, there,' he called. 'I'm sure as hell glad to see you.'

The girl was silhouetted against the blue of the sky. Jason took a sharp breath, thinking how magnificent she looked. She wore a split riding skirt with a white blouse and blue jacket.

'I could do with a little help,' he said. 'I got two wounded men here an' I gotta get them to the doc afore one o' them bleeds to death.'

Grace raised her eyebrows and slid easily to the ground. 'Knew there'd be trouble first time I laid eyes on you.'

She didn't ask what had happened even when she saw who the wounded men were, but ripped strips from their shirts to bind their wounds. 'Better get going,' she said. 'Duke's bleeding bad.'

With the help of Grace's companion, who was later introduced as Lew, Jason laid the two men on the back of the buggy. Lew watched over them as they set off along the trail to Inspiration at a good pace. Jason, leading the two spare horses, followed.

The good folk of Inspiration were well used to seeing injured men being taken through the town but showed increased interest when they recognized who these men were.

Grace stopped outside Doc MacReady's house and hammered on the door.

'He's good at his job,' Grace told Jason before the door was flung open.

The doc was an amiable man, past middle age and with a liking for good food and fine drink. This was evident in the spread of his stomach and the red flush of his nose and cheeks. His hands, however, were delicate, the fingers long.

He urged them inside as soon as he saw that his medical skills were required, Jason carrying Duke with some difficulty and Zeb managing on his own. They were led into the doc's surgery, a room at the back of the house which smelled of carbolic and another odour that Jason couldn't place. Duke was laid on a cot covered with a white sheet while Zeb was seated in a chair.

The doc bent and examined his patient. Then he turned to Zeb. 'You can wait. This one's urgent.' He ushered Jason and Grace out. 'Leave this to me. I'll let yer know how it goes.'

'How bad is it, doc?' Jason asked.

The doc looked up. 'He's not gonna die, if that's what you mean. He'll be back at work tomorrow but he won't be breakin' in no broncos fer a while.' He waved them away.

'Well?' Grace asked when they were outside. 'Reckon it's time you told me what happened.'

Before Jason could explain they were faced with the angry figure of the sheriff. 'Saw you ride in,' he said. 'Knew you'd be trouble.'

Jason shrugged. 'Seems to be the general opinion.'

'Go sit yerself in my office an' wait fer me. I'm gonna get to the bottom o' this.' He rapped on the doc's door. 'First I'm gonna see what's goin' on in here.'

'I ain't about to go nowhere,' Jason said.

'See yer don't.' The sheriff turned. 'You, too, Grace. I want your side o' the story.'

'Not much to tell,' Grace said.

While they sat in the sheriff's office Jason told Grace everything, how he had managed to turn the tables on the two polecats who had threatened him.

As he talked he watched Grace's

reactions and was impressed by the fact that she hadn't so far blamed him for the trouble.

'Duke's an angry man,' Jason finished. 'I was hopin' to patch up our little difference of opinion but it seems he's otherwise minded.'

'I tried to warn you,' Grace said. 'You've made enemies for life. If you're still of a mind to work for my pa I wish you luck. You'll need it.'

Kelly Quintock returned and threw himself into the leather chair behind his desk. He gave a deep sigh and fired a cigar, peering closely at Jason through the smoke.

'I've bin in this job too long. I got so I kin smell trouble afore it arrives. An' I could smell it on you.'

'That's the third time I've bin told that,' Jason said. 'I'm gettin' a mite sick on it. Truth is, trouble found me.'

'Well,' the sheriff began, 'whichever way round it might be seems like you've earned a place in the cells. Lucky it's not the gallows. I've spoke to Zeb an' he's told me how you bushwhacked the two o' them out on the trail. What fer would you do that?'

Jason leapt to his feet. 'The devil you say! I was held up by those two varmints. They were goin' to hogtie me. What they had in mind after that I don't know an' I don't think I wanna know.'

'Hold yer horses. Look at it my way. There's two men with slugs in 'em and you with not a scratch. Until I kin talk to Duke an' make sense outa all this I need to keep you where I kin see you.' He looked at Grace. 'What d'you know about this?'

Grace hesitated. 'Not much, Sheriff. I was riding into town for supplies and I heard shooting. Two shots. I wouldn't think on telling you your job but you might have a look at the three six-guns, see how many slugs've been fired. Jason's Colt was on the floor when I got there which might mean they took it from him.'

The sheriff laughed. 'Perhaps you should be wearin' the star. D'ya think I haven't thought of that? Anyways, there's bin plenty of time for the evidence to be messed up.'

'Sorry, Sheriff. Just trying to be helpful. Though, if you ask me, they were both askin' for it. You know what they're like.'

'Reckon I do. But I haven't yet got a tag on this man here. And, until I do, he's gonna spend a night in the back.' He gestured with his thumb in the direction of the cells. 'Mind you, there's only two cells and one's already occupied. Any drunks tonight'll have to share.' A grin told Jason that the sheriff was enjoying this.

Trying to hold his anger in check Jason said, 'You've no cause to lock me up, Sheriff. If you want me I'll be out at the CB Ranch. If you feel the need to fill your cells I suggest you put Zeb and Duke in there soon as they've bin patched up.'

The sheriff leaned forward until Jason found himself staring into his bloodshot eyes. 'I've just about had a bellyful. I'm wearin' the badge. I'm putting you behind bars and that's an end to it.'

'I guess I don't have a choice,' Jason said. Although he was resigned to being locked up he realized that perhaps this might provide him with an opportunity to question young Billy Manning about the outlaw, Adam One-ear.

His only concern was that his version of the events would almost certainly be contradicted by the other two men and he would be in no position to do anything about it.

The sheriff rose. 'Thanks, Grace. I won't be troublin' you no more.'

As Grace made for the door she said over her shoulder to Jason, 'I'll take your horse to the livery and I'll tell Pa what's happened. And I'll send you in some grub. As sure as there's cows on the prairie the sheriff here won't be obliging you.'

The sheriff said nothing and waited until she had left the office; then he beckoned to Jason and took a bunch of

71

keys from the desk drawer. 'Let's go.'

The cell into which Jason was pushed was far from clean. A metal cot, covered by a thin mattress and blanket, was fixed to the wall. A bucket sat under a shelf on which there was a tin mug and a jug. The water in the jug had a layer of dust on its surface.

'Bring the food in soon as it arrives,' Jason said. 'I'm kinda hungry.'

That brought a grunt of derision. 'Serving meals ain't part of the service. Mebbe you'll get it and mebbe you won't. I might take a fancy to it myself.'

Jason gave a tight grin. 'That's remarkable hospitable of you, Sheriff.'

'Think nothing of it.' Kelly Quintock seemed satisfied with his day's work as he slammed the cell door shut and returned to the office.

All this time Billy Manning in the adjacent cell had watched in sullen silence.

'You eaten anything?' Jason asked.

Billy leaned back on his bunk and said nothing.

'Cos if you haven't you kin share mine if an' when it comes.'

This offer brought no response and Jason wondered if he was going to get any information at all. He tried again. 'For all you have a grievance agin this town and Carter Brown, hitchin' up with a killer like Adam One-ear is gonna do you no favours.'

Thinking he saw some reaction in Billy's eyes he continued, 'If you're minded to choose the path of an outlaw or a gunslinger there'll be no way back.' The hard steel of his eyes fixed on the young man, holding his attention. 'An outlaw's profession has only one end. You'll either have a rope round yer neck or a slug in yer guts. Either way you'll end up dead.'

Billy rose to the bait. 'Adam's worth six of anyone in this town. He helped me after I'd bin thrown by my horse. No need to do it. Coulda left me but he didn't.'

Jason nodded. 'I'd like to meet him. I think he saved my life, too,' he said.

Billy gave this some thought. 'Yeah, that figures. I've bin a lotta things since Pa died, cowhand, bar-room swamper, even did shotgun once. Now I'm gonna be an outlaw.' He said this proudly.

He was about to go on when the sheriff appeared again. He rattled the keys outside Billy's cell door. 'Hope you haven't made yersel' too comfortable,' he said. 'I've decided mebbe to let you go.'

Billy leaped to his feet. 'What the hell does that mean, Sheriff? Mebbe?'

'It means it depends. I've made some enquiries. Your family was well respected round these parts. Anyways, I'll be needin' the cell tonight. But you'll have to give me an undertaking that you'll not think of doin' nothing foolish again.'

'Agreed,' Billy said and gave a knowing wink to Jason.

'And 'cos I don't reckon you're a real outlaw.' The sheriff smirked. 'Mebbe you'd like to be but you're still wet behind the ears.'

The younger man was stung. 'You're

last year's lawman! I'm nearly eighteen years old. I kin outthink you, outrun you and outdraw you. I'll bet you haven't arrested a real hardcase fer a long, long time.'

The sheriff had not yet unlocked the cell door. He rattled the keys again. 'You're not goin' the best way about it if you want to git outa here. I've a mind to leave you till you get a civil tongue in yer head.'

'Time you retired, Sheriff, an' gave yer job to a younger man. Now, d'ya mind bringin' me somethin' to fill my belly an' let me eat it in peace.'

To Jason's surprise the sheriff placed the key in the lock and swung the cell door open, beckoning Billy out. 'You're gettin' no grub here. You've outstayed yer welcome. Get going afore I arrest you again. Go an' see if your outlaw friend'll take you under his wing. I'm sure you'll be a great asset to him an' his gang.' His derision was barely concealed.

The sheriff looked hard at Jason.

'You'll be stayin'. I've had a word with the two men you bushwhacked. Your story doesn't hold up. Prepare yerself fer a long stay.'

Jason grabbed the bars. 'What I told you was the truth!' Not only was he being denied the chance to find out about Adam One-ear, his freedom was also being taken from him. And it occurred to him that the sheriff might be giving Billy his freedom so that he would lead him unwittingly to the outlaw's hideout.

'Watch yer back, Billy,' he called as they went through into the office and the intervening door slammed shut. 'Dammit to hell,' he muttered. 'Someone's gonna pay when I get out of here.' But he was less than certain that he would.

* * *

'Why're you really lettin' me go, Sheriff?' Billy asked when he was seated in the chair facing Quintock.

'I told ya. I deal with dangerous varmints in this town every day an' I don't want my time taken up dealing with the likes of you. You're no more than a stone in my boot. Now, are ya goin' or not? If you take my advice you'll high-tail it outa this town an' get as far away from Adam One-ear as you can. An outlaw's life is very short.'

Billy needed no further encouragement. 'I'll not be takin' your advice, Sheriff. I'll be more welcome in the gang than I am here, fer sure.' He levered himself off the chair. 'Now I'll be needing my hardware that you took from me. And I'll want some cash to pay the livery fer stabling my horse,' he added, knowing that he had plenty of paper money tucked in his boot.

The sheriff sighed. 'You're a persistent cuss, ain't ya?' He opened the desk drawer, withdrew Billy's gunbelt and handed it to him.

'An' the rifle.'

The sheriff hesitated before unlocking the chain and taking the Winchester from the rack. 'You kin have yer artillery but I'm not letting you outa here with slugs. You'll have to buy them if you think you need any. And you ain't gettin' no dollars from me. Go.' He took hold of the younger man's arm and pushed him out into the street. 'And don't come back!'

All this talking had given Billy time to think. While he bought ammunition and retrieved his horse he pondered on the situation. He didn't trust the sheriff's motives for giving him his freedom and had arrived at the conclusion that the law, in the form of Kelly Quintock, was certain to be on his tail.

He stayed long enough to buy himself a meal before setting off back up the trail on which he had arrived. There was only an hour or two before sundown.

He glanced back several times as he put distance between himself and the town and began to relax when he saw nothing to cause him any trouble. It was when he stopped at a small rill to allow his horse to drink that he spotted a movement about half a mile behind. He watched without allowing himself to be seen and was rewarded by the brief sight of a rider slipping into the cover of some trees. He thought he saw movement further back still, but dismissed the idea.

He smiled. Now he could have some fun. He took false trails, especially where the terrain was particularly rocky and he could conceal himself so that the sheriff would think he'd lost him. Then, suddenly, Billy would reappear further down, allowing the lawman to get sight of him, for he was certain he knew who was trailing him. He was confident in the belief that the lawman had no intention of shooting him. Yet. Not until he had led him to the Redford gang.

'C'mon, you ugly critter,' he muttered. 'You helped drive my family outa their farm an' now it's your turn to pay the price.' Did the old fool think he was invisible?

He rode until the sun dipped behind the mountains to the west, then stopped among a clump of willow at the edge of a small creek where he could settle comfortably for the night. As he ate his supper of biscuits, bacon and coffee heated over a small fire he hoped the sheriff was far less comfortable. He warmed himself by the flickering flames and smiled in the knowledge that the sheriff would not have risked lighting a fire.

Night had settled through the trees and lay like a blanket over the landscape. The fire crackled and in his mind he saw himself as he had been only eight short years ago, when he had camped with his pa and they had all been content in their homestead, looking forward to the future. That was then. The sheriff and the rancher, Carter Brown, had ended their dream and they would both pay, the sheriff first. And soon.

He owed nobody nothing. Except Adam One-ear, who had taken him into the outlaw gang, young and inexperienced as he was, and had given him the chance to prove himself. Well, he wasn't about to let his new friend down again.

He slept well and, at sunup, ate a casual breakfast of beans and bread. The aroma of the freshly made coffee rose into the still air and he was almost tempted to offer a mug to the sheriff. The thought appealed to him, but he wasn't ready yet to let him know that he was aware of his presence. He would do so when it was time for the man to take his knowledge to the grave.

He cleaned his mug and cooking-pans, dowsed the fire and kicked dirt over the embers. Then, refreshed, he saddled up and sprang into the saddle. He checked the rifle and the Colt at his hip and set off with a smile on his face. Soon he would need to pick a spot for the ambush.

He was surprised later when he saw riders emerge from behind a large outcrop and recognized them as two members of the Redford gang, Jo-Jo Logan, small and wiry with a permanent sneer, and Frankie Smith, powerfully built with a face full of whiskers. These were the two outlaws who had shown the least enthusiasm when Adam took him in. They were dressed alike in blue pants, grey shirt and vest and black Stetsons.

They reined in on either side of him. 'What're you doin' in this neck of the woods?' Jo-Jo growled. 'Thought you was robbin' a bank or something.' He gave Billy a hard look.

'I was,' Billy said. 'Well, almost.'

Frankie gave a belly laugh. 'Whadya mean, almost? I don't cotton to mysteries. You either did or you didn't.'

'I mean I nearly did. Some polecat stopped me.'

Jo-Jo raised his eyebrows. 'Adam'll sure be pleased to hear that. He'll be proud of ya. You nearly robbed a bank!

That's good! Well, you best ride on an' tell him.'

Billy shook his head. 'Can't do that. Got somethin' to do first.'

'An' what's so all-fired important that we can't do it fer ya?'

'A *hombre's* bin trailin' me. I'm gonna put a slug in him.' He withdrew the rifle from its scabbard.

Jo-Jo screwed up his eyes and peered into the distance. 'Cain't see nothing.'

'He's there. Bin following me fer quite a ways. Thinks he's invisible cos he's got a star on his vest.'

'A star?'

'Yeah, the sheriff.'

Frankie thrust out his hand and grabbed Billy by the arm. 'You stupid or something?'

Billy shrugged him off angrily. 'I was havin' a bit of fun with him, is all. He sure as hell ain't going no place now.'

'You're damn right he ain't goin' nowhere. But you're not gonna do it. Leave that to us. We won't be makin' no mistakes.'

Billy opened his mouth to protest when Frankie gave his horse a sharp slap on its hindquarters. 'Go tell Adam what we're doin'. You'll find him at the hideout with the rest of the gang.'

Billy reluctantly set off but not before he heard Jo-Jo mutter savagely, 'Dunno what got into Adam, takin' in a lame-brain like that.'

He turned in the saddle and watched as the two outlaws circled back and lay in wait for the sheriff.

He had no doubt they would succeed in what they planned to do.

6

The night passed slowly for Jason. The deputy sheriff brought him the food that Grace had promised and he had water to drink. A whiskey or a cold beer would have been acceptable but those were not on offer.

Early next day he had a visitor. He had expected, and maybe hoped, that it would be Grace, but he recognized the voice of Carter Brown and another man raised in anger before the inner door opened.

The rancher entered, followed by a deputy sheriff whom Jason had not seen before. He was fresh-faced, maybe in his middle twenties with a silver star prominent on his shirt. Jason guessed this was Kelly Quintock's deputy, Fletcher, who was now attempting to hide his indecision in the face of the older man's determined manner.

'I can't let him go unless Kelly says so,' Fletcher was saying. 'He told me to keep an eye on him.'

The rancher set his jaw. 'Goddamn it, Fletcher, I just about pay your wages. To hell with what you were told, now I'm tellin' ya. Open up. I'll guarantee your prisoner won't run away.'

'But . . . '

'Where is the sheriff, anyway?'

Fletcher shrugged. 'Dunno. He took off in a kinda hurry just after he let his other prisoner go.'

Carter Brown grabbed the bunch of keys from the desk and thrust them out. 'Well, now I'm lettin' this prisoner loose. Get him.'

Fletcher's resistance ended, and without another word he fetched Jason from the cell.

'Come with me,' Carter ordered and went to the door. Then he turned. 'Tell Kelly I want to see him as soon as he returns,' he said. 'When he gets back he knows where to find me. Meantime my daughter's gone missing. I want you to gather up some men an' ride out to the ranch. We're gonna look for her. Now give this man his gunbelt back and move aside.' To Jason he said, 'Help me on to my horse.'

Jason shrugged, picked up his possessions and went after him. He pulled open the door and they stepped out into the heat of the morning.

When they were both in the saddle the rancher sagged. 'We've got some hard riding to do. We've gotta find her.'

As they left the town behind them Carter Brown briefly described the situation. 'I've got all available men out looking. You've not done me any favours by shooting up Zeb and Duke.'

It was not easy to hold a conversation while they were moving at a fast pace and Jason held back on saying much.

As they eased their mounts and rode alongside each other on the trail the rancher asked, 'You saw Grace last night. What exactly did she say to you?'

'Nothing in partic'lar? How long's she bin gone?'

'She didn't come home last night. Must've gone somewhere just after she left you. She's wild but never scares us like this.'

'Might she've bin thrown?'

'Possible, though she's as skilled on horseback as any man. Better'n most.'

'What d'you want me to do?'

'Join the search. That's all. If you find anything, three even shots, then three more. She never strays outside the ranch and we know the rides she's fond of taking. So we've divided the area up into sections, two men to a section. When we get to the ranch you'll be told where to go and who'll partner you. You'll be needing some sort of guidance, you not being familiar with the terrain. I was hoping to involve the sheriff but he's missing just when he's needed. Fletcher's still chewin' with his milk teeth.'

Jason considered what he'd been told. He recognized, even from his brief acquaintance with the rancher's daughter, that she was both competent and headstrong.

He also had an idea why the sheriff was absent and why he had released Billy Manning. He would now be on the younger man's trail. What he could expect to achieve by going alone, if indeed he had, was doubtful.

Altogether Jason was now convinced that, when he had entered Inspiration, he had walked into a complex web of intrigue and danger. For a brief moment he considered whether he should just high-tail out away from the place but the thought was swiftly pushed aside. A girl was in trouble out there somewhere and no red-blooded man would leave her to her fate. The fact that it was the lovely Grace had nothing to do with it.

He received his instructions from one of the cowpokes who had been given the task of organising the search. He was pleased that he was to be accompanied by Lew, the wrangler who had helped him before.

The area Jason had been given was studded with hills, creeks, stands of trees, low brush, boulders and gullies and he soon realized the magnitude of the task. If Grace had been thrown from her horse she could be anywhere and almost invisible. Her pinto, however, would be more easily seen.

They rode carefully, criss-crossing the ground, peering into the most obvious places, but they saw nothing. It was while they shared a drink of water from a canteen that Jason gleaned a little more of the activities of the ranch and its owner, Carter Brown.

'You gonna work fer the CB?' Lew asked suddenly.

'Yeah, that's the idea,' Jason said. 'Till I can gather a stake together, an' then I'll probably be off again.'

Lew seemed to hesitate, then blurted out, 'Might be a good idea.'

Jason didn't immediately understand what Lew was trying to tell him. He waited for more.

'Last man to come to work here disappeared,' Lew continued.

'What? Just high-tailed out?'

'Nope. Least, I don't think so.'

But, even under questioning, Lew would say no more and they continued their search.

Two hours into it they began to think that this was a waste of time and hoped that others would be more successful. An hour later they hadn't found Grace. But Jason found the sheriff. The lawman's horse was contentedly eating the grass in a sheltered area at the foot of a sharp escarpment. A little further on Jason saw the law officer's body sprawled face up on the ground.

He slid from the saddle and knelt beside the inert form. Fearing that the sheriff was dead, he soon established that the man was very much alive but unconscious.

He examined him carefully but could see no obvious injury and certainly no telltale holes where slugs might have entered. If the man had been thrown

Jason could see no rocks or other hard objects that could have knocked him out.

'What in tarnation are you doin' this far outa yer bailiwick?' Jason muttered.

It was when he turned the body over that he saw the bloody groove in the sheriff's scalp. The hairs pricked on the back of his neck and he swiftly swept his gaze over the surrounding area. Out here, without cover, he was a sitting target if the shooter was still there.

He saw nothing, but remained alert and called Lew.

'Some varmint bushwhacked him,' he said.

Lew walked over to the sheriff's horse, talking quietly all the time. He rubbed his hand over the grey's flank. 'She's bin run hard,' he announced and examined the animal more closely. 'There's blood on the cantle. I think the sheriff was shot some way back and managed to hang on. He was leaning forward afore he fell.' This was a long speech for Lew and Jason grinned.

'Leastwise it looks as if he was a mite lucky.' He lifted the sheriff's head up and trickled some water into his mouth.

The sheriff groaned and coughed and opened his eyes. His lips moved but the words that came out were disjointed and difficult to understand.

'Take it easy,' Jason told him. 'You've bin shot. We'll get you back to the ranch and have the doc look at you.'

'I'm OK,' Quintock mumbled. 'They don't kill me as easy as that.' His hand went up to his scalp. 'I was trailin' the kid,' he whispered. 'Then I saw 'em comin' at me. Thought I'd got away an' then Grace . . . ' His voice became weaker, his eyes closed and his head sank back.

Although he rallied a little after another mouthful of water he could say no more, leaving Jason to ponder who could have been chasing him. The answer would clearly have to wait until the man had received medical attention.

'I'll take him back to the ranch,' Lew

said. 'Best sit him up front o' me.' He led the grey over and tied its reins to his cantle. Between them they hoisted the sheriff on to Lew's mount, where he sat slumped and all but unconscious.

Jason was glad to go along with this arrangement. 'I'll continue the search for Grace,' he said. But what did he expect to find?

While Lew made a covering for the sheriff's head and set off, Jason cast about for tracks. It seemed reasonable to suppose that the lawman, when he tumbled from his horse, would have been riding away from trouble and towards the ranch or the town. He took a line from that general direction and mentally extended it backwards. He was no tracker but the signs were clear enough in parts and he set off to follow them, hoping that this might lead him to the girl. For a while the tracks in the clay were obvious but as the surface hardened tracking became more difficult.

He had been studying the ground for

about half an hour and was so intent that he failed to see the approaching rider. When he did finally look up it was too late to take evasive action, he withdrew his Winchester from its scabbard and held it ready with the butt against his thigh.

The horse wheeled to a stop beside him but by this time he had recognized the rider. 'Grace, there're men out searching for you!' he grated. 'Your pa's worried to hell an' back.' He looked at the pinto. 'Why're you in such a hell-fire hurry?'

She turned in the saddle and pointed. From around a bluff about a quarter of a mile away two horsemen had appeared, moving fast.

'What in tarnation?' Jason growled. He screwed up his eyes against the glare.

'That's why I was hurrying,' Grace told him, anger giving her voice a sharp edge. 'I was trying to get away from them.'

Jason looked around. 'Well, they're

gonna get more than they expected. Quick. We're kinda in the open here.' He guided his horse behind a large outcrop of rock, slid from the saddle. 'We'll find out how determined they are.'

He turned his head to see that Grace had also grabbed her rifle and was steadying it on a ledge.

'Let me do the shootin' unless they want to take us on,' he said. Grace said nothing.

As the riders approached he fired two shots, both kicking up the dust in front of their mounts. They hauled on the reins, wheeled and circled, drew their Colts and searched for a target.

'That's far enough,' Jason roared. He fired twice more, again aiming low, spooking the horses. 'If you wanna make a fight of it go ahead. Otherwise put ya guns away an' go back where ya came from.'

The men, who obviously had not expected such opposition, holstered their weapons. One touched the brim of his hat. 'Jest having a bit o' fun,' he called, and led the other away.

It soon became obvious that they hadn't gone far and what their intention was. A rifle cracked and a bullet drew splinters of rock inches from Jason's head. He threw himself sideways, taking Grace with him as other shots followed the first.

'The varmints've got round behind us,' Jason growled. They rolled into the cover of a projecting rock and considered the situation.

He nodded at Grace's rifle. 'You any good with that?'

'Fair,' she said.

'Well, it's two against two. I don't fancy their chances. Keep 'em occupied while I circle around. We'll soon have 'em flushed out.'

Grace fired off a few rounds as Jason moved off to the left, keeping to the shelter of the large boulders that lay scattered on the ground.

There was enough cover among the stunted trees clawing into the rocks for him to circle the shooters' position without being seen, and he began to inch his way towards them. With nothing to fire at their guns were silent and Jason couldn't be sure exactly where they were. He removed his Stetson, placed it carefully on a boulder with the crown showing, then moved five swift paces to his right.

He was rewarded with an immediate shot; his hat spun off and he grinned that such a simple ruse should bring results. He risked a swift glance above the rock and spotted the telltale puff of smoke that told him that the man was no more than twenty yards away.

He picked up a loose rock and tossed it to his right. As the shooter fired Jason moved, catlike, further to his left, up and around the line of outcrops, and was rewarded with a side view of one of the men who was kneeling with his rifle rested on a ledge. It was pointing in the wrong direction.

'Shuck yer guns,' he roared.

The men whirled and loosed off

some wild shots.

Jason raised his rifle and fired. The slug caught one man in the upper part of his arm. He yelled an oath and fell back, dropping his weapon as he did so.

The second man, seeing where the shot had come from, opened up with a volley, unwisely showing himself above his shelter. Grace's rifle spat, and he too fell into the dirt.

Jason stood up and walked towards them, his rifle held ready and his finger on the trigger. Both men were alive, although the one Grace had shot, the smaller of the two with the sneer fixed on his face, seemed to be badly injured. To Jason's keen eyes they did not appear to be cowpunchers but dyed-in-the-wool gunfighters, dressed as they were in blue pants and grey shirts and with bandannas around their necks. Six-guns nestled at their hips, the holsters tied down.

'What fer didn't you leave when ya had the chance?' he demanded. 'You'd no need to attack us.'

'Goddamn it!' one swore. 'We was after the woman. She'd bin spying on us.'

'I doubt that,' Jason said as Grace joined him. 'More likely the other way round. How bad are ya hurt?'

'Bad enough,' the large man said. Rage contorted his whiskery features.

'Well,' Jason grated, 'we'll take you back with us, see what the sheriff says.'

To his surprise Grace shook her head. 'Let them go,' she said. 'It'll be more trouble than it's worth.'

Jason was intrigued to learn where the men had come from. As far as he knew there was empty prairie for fifty miles. 'I reckon you should have yer wounds seen to,' he told them. He gestured with his thumb. 'Who's gonna help you back there?'

'None o' yer business.'

Jason hesitated and looked questioningly at Grace. He made up his mind. 'Please yerselves. Leave yer weapons on the ground an' be on yer way.'

Once all their guns were safely

stowed at Grace's feet he helped hoist the more severely wounded man on to his horse. 'I think you're making a mistake,' he told them. 'He's bleedin' bad.'

The man stretched his mouth into a grin. 'It's you that's makin' the mistake,' he yelled as they rode off.

Jason watched them until they were out of sight. He pointed to Grace's rifle. 'Was that a lucky shot of yours just now?'

By way of an answer she picked up a small piece of rock and threw it high, levered a shell into the breech, brought her Winchester up to her shoulder and fired. The rock shattered before reaching the ground.

'Impressive,' Jason acknowledged, gazing at her with admiration. 'Sorry I doubted you. You can sure handle it.'

'Men!' Grace said with a half-smile. 'They believe they're the only ones who can handle firearms. I've been brought up to take care of myself.'

'I can see you didn't really need me

here,' he said with a grin.

'Hmm. I'm grateful you showed up when you did.'

'Why were those men after you?' he asked.

'They were chasing the sheriff at first, then they transferred their attentions on to me.'

'Did they put a slug in him or was it you?'

Grace shook her head and her long hair spun round her shoulders. 'No, it was most certainly not me,' she said angrily. 'I heard shooting and saw some riders. I hid until they left. I saw the sheriff ridin' like the wind, coming this way.

'I lost him. I think he stopped a slug by the way he was slumped. We'll have to go and find him.'

'No need,' Jason told her. 'I'll explain everything on the way back to the ranch. And you can tell me what in hell you were thinking of, riding out here alone.' He fired three shots into the air and then another three.

'If they heard that they'll know you're safe,' he said and turned his horse. 'Let's take the good news to your pa.'

To his surprise Grace said, 'No hurry. We can take our time.'

Jason raised his eyebrows, retrieved his hat, now with a neat hole in the crown, and climbed into the saddle.

★ ★ ★

After Billy had reluctantly left the two hardcases to deal with the sheriff, he made his way to the hideout. He rode disconsolately, nursing the hate he felt for those who had harmed his family.

His heart sank a little as he approached the hidden caves where his new friends hung out. In fact only Adam had shown him any friendship. The others had accepted him with shrugs of their shoulders, seeing this fresh-faced boy as a liability rather than a valued member. It was Adam who had found him lying unconscious, and it was Adam who had given him the

103

opportunity to prove himself by robbing the bank in Inspiration.

Billy had failed in that and now he had failed again in killing the sheriff. He realized it had been unwise of him to lure the man but it had been his intention that the sheriff would not be returning.

'I'll show 'em all yet,' he muttered to himself.

The hideout, approached over rocky ground, was a naturally concealed system of caves and open grassland, entered through an opening in a fold of the massive rocks that appeared, even close to, as no opening at all and was shielded by a line of pines.

Billy guided his horse through the trees, skirted the loose boulders and turned into the narrow fissure. After fifty yards the space between the high, red cliff sides opened out to reveal two wooden buildings, a corral and, beyond, a large area of grassy plain. A lazy stream, fed from the rocks above, meandered away from him.

The five men sitting outside the huts gave him scant attention. These, together with Adam and the two he had just left made up the entire gang. They had worked together for six years, robbing and killing over a wide area, until the bounty that had been put on their heads was becoming a hindrance.

Billy made for the larger of the huts where he knew he would find Adam, who looked up as he entered. 'How'd ya get on at the bank?' he asked.

'Didn't make it,' Billy admitted. His eyes shifted left and right, seeking a way out of his embarrassment.

'So I heard.' Adam roared with laughter. He was all of six feet, fit-looking with muscles visible under his check shirt. His grey eyes were deep and unreadable. A heavy moustache adorned his upper lip and long, black hair hid his missing ear.

'Weren't my fault. Some varmint thought he was savin' my hide. Called the sheriff.'

'Yeah, I heard it went something like

that.' Adam slapped Billy on the back. 'You had a spell in jail, too, so I bin told. Won't do you no harm.'

The younger man gritted his teeth, knowing that Adam was quietly laughing at him. 'I'm glad the sheriff's dead,' he grunted and then realized he'd said too much.

Adam appraised him with a new expression. 'How'd ya know that? Did you kill him? 'Cos if you did I'll revise my opinion of you. Long as you didn't shoot him in the back. Wouldn't like that.'

'I would've put some lead in him if I'd bin left to it,' Billy started to explain, and he went on to tell Adam what had happened. 'Anyway, he'll be eatin' dust now so that'll save me the bother.'

'Where?'

Billy wondered how far he could go in avoiding the truth, realizing that the two outlaws would be returning soon and would be happy to recount the true story. 'On the way here,' he said. 'I was playin' with him, lettin' him think I was leading him on.'

Adam's face darkened. 'I don't believe you were thinkin' at all. What if you'd led him far enough to know where to find us?'

'Well, I didn't, did I?' Billy turned on his heel.

'Wait!' Adam called him back. 'For now I don't want you wanderin' off on your own. You've a lot to learn. You're to stay here until I tell you otherwise. Is that clear? I took you in and I can just as easily get rid of you. Understood?'

Billy nodded sullenly. Adam had made it all too plain.

His situation worsened when the two outlaws, Jo-Jo and Frankie, returned weaponless and explained that the sheriff had escaped, that they had been attacked and wounded by a stranger and a girl, the daughter of the local rancher.

'You let him get away!' Adam roared.
'We got off a couple of shots and

may've killed him,' the smaller man said.

'But ya don't know?' Adam shrugged. 'You're not much better than he is.' He pointed to Billy. 'Now get outa my sight. All o' ya.'

7

Jason and Grace took the journey slowly, partly because Grace needed to rest her horse and partly because Jason dictated the pace in the hope of learning more about how the sheriff got shot. For the first ten minutes they rode in silence. Jason waited patiently and enjoyed the familiar scents of the prairie and the woods, the grasses, pine and cattle brought to him on the slight breeze. He could sense that the girl was troubled, maybe turning over in her mind how much she could trust him and what she could tell him.

Then suddenly, by the banks of a fast-flowing creek, she reined in the pinto and waited for Jason to do the same. They faced each other and the silence lengthened.

'Aren't you curious?' she asked, her voice low.

He smiled. 'About what?'

'About . . . everything.'

'I'm puzzled about many things,' he admitted. 'But just now I reckon we'd best get you back to the ranch.' He glanced at the sky. 'I think there's a storm coming. Your pa'll be anxious.'

'It'll do him good to worry a piece.'

'If that's how you see it.' Nevertheless he fired three more shots into the air, followed by a further three and was relieved to hear the answering shots he was hoping for.

'OK, so I'm curious. About what the sheriff was up to, why your pa offered me a job, what Zeb an' Duke have agin me, where the outlaw gang might be holed up. And, yep, I'm mightily interested in you and where you fit in. Seems to me there's something going on round here that involves me and I'd surely like to know what it is.'

Grace looked thoughtful. 'I haven't got the answers to all your questions. I tried to warn you when we first met that you had to be careful. It might've bin better for you to hit the trail right then. But here you are and I guess you've decided to stick around.'

'Kinda looks that way.' Jason slid to the ground and stretched, trailing the reins so that his horse could feed on the rich pasture and drink from the cool water. 'What *do* you know?' He sat on a rock and threw stones into the stream.

She dismounted and sat next to him. They stayed close together but not quite touching for several minutes. Jason turned his head to look at and admire her while her eyes remained fixed on the horizon. A man could settle down with such a girl. She had beauty and spirit, yet somehow seemed vulnerable.

Then she said, 'I know that Pa's short of cash. Yeah, it's a big ranch but there's bin problems with cattle rustling, drought and disease that's set him back some. But there's something else. I'm not sure what it is but Zeb's got something to do with it. And my pa, I think.'

'Your pa gave me a job and enough dollars to buy these clothes. He knew nothing about me. Why would he do that?'

'I've been wondering that. He thinks he needs you. What particular skills d'you have?'

Jason smiled. 'Nothin' out o' the ordinary.'

'You're not the usual gunslinger type, hired for your gun, are you?'

'Nope. I told your pa that.'

They lapsed into silence again until Grace said, 'You have to watch your back. There's something going on I don't understand.'

'Well,' Jason drawled, 'there's no shortage of people willing to give me a warning. Thanks for your advice, Grace. The rest is up to me.'

'Duke needs watching but Zeb's more dangerous. He leads, Duke follows. You don't know what you're up against. And neither do I.'

'Mebbe not, but you can tell me everything you do know. Such as what you were doing when you were chased by those two *hombres*. You were a long way from home.'

She laid a hand on his arm and he felt an unexpected thrill. 'I'm obliged. Really I am. I like to ride in the evening. I love that time of day when the light begins to fade. I feel free. I was minding my own business when I caught sight of the sheriff moving cautiously. I thought maybe he was trailing someone so I followed him. He didn't see me and I camped when he did.'

'You camped overnight? That was a mite . . . ' He was about to say foolish, so he finished lamely, ' . . . daring.'

'Yep, but I did it anyway. Pa always insisted that I carry enough food and water when I go riding, so that wasn't a problem. I managed to follow for a while this morning but I lost him. Later I heard shooting so I pulled into shelter and waited. Then I saw a rider coming round the bluff at full gallop and recognized the sheriff. He was bent forward, sort of slumped, holding on as best he could.

'I started after him but those two other riders spotted me and turned in my direction. They didn't look like they were friendly. I wasn't going to hang around to find out what they wanted so I sent a couple of shots in their direction to warn them off.'

'And did it?'

'You know the answer to that one. It held them back for a while, that's all.'

'Did Kelly see you?'

'I don't think so. He was too out of it to do anything anyway.'

'Sort of lucky I came along.'

'Yep. I sure owe you.'

'Do you know who they were?'

'No. The sheriff may have recognized them. We'll have to ask him.'

They lapsed once more into silence, each lost in thoughts of their own. Here, in the shade of the willow, they were screened briefly from the intrigue and danger that had been their companions. Jason felt relaxed, sensing an intimacy developing between them. He took a breath to speak but the words wouldn't come. Now was not the time.

Too soon, they remounted and left the peaceful scene reluctantly. It took them another two hours to reach the ranch.

★   ★   ★

As the light faded Carter Brown, seated on the veranda, watched their approach with a broad smile. As they drew near he called, 'I knew I'd made the right judgement of you.'

'What was all the fuss?' Grace asked. She dismounted and submitted to a long hug from her pa. 'I was only out ridin'.'

The rancher kept his arm around her and turned to Jason. 'Grace knows better'n to stay out overnight. Reckon you've earned yourself a good meal and strong drink. Come and join us if you will.' He signalled to a young man who seemed to be busy doing nothing. 'Take care of their horses, Sam. Real good care.'

'How's the sheriff?' Jason asked.

'Feelin' better. The doc should be here any time now but Kelly's an ornery cuss. Keeps yellin' fer his clothes. We think he oughta rest after that blow on the head but mebbe his skull is thicker than most. I'll take you up later. He wants to thank whoever found him. I guess that's you.'

Jason nodded. 'He sort of found me.'

'And then you found Grace.'

'It's bin a busy day.'

'I'm mightily obliged to you.'

The rancher was helped to his feet and led them into the house, through the entrance hall and into a large room fitted out with leather-bound arm-chairs, shelves of books and cabinets holding glass and silverware. Full-length curtains framed the windows that gave a view of the yard and beyond. A crystal chandelier hung centrally above a round oak table and a thick carpet covered the floor. A longcase clock, a handsome mahogany desk and a locked gun cabinet stood against the walls.

It was an impressive room, conveying good taste. Jason took time to allow his gaze to appreciate what he was seeing. If the whole house was furnished in a similar fashion either Carter Brown was a very rich man or had been at one time. Certainly a man who seemed to enjoy wealth.

'Whiskey?' the rancher asked when they were seated. He motioned to Grace and she opened a cabinet and poured a good measure of pale liquid into four glasses.

The mystery of who the fourth glass was for was solved when Zeb entered the room. He was obviously still in pain, with his arm strapped up. He stopped in the doorway and glared at Jason. Their eyes held each other, Jason's curious, Zeb's with naked hatred.

'Now,' Carter Brown said as if he

hadn't noticed the charged atmosphere. 'We'll get to the bottom of this. Grace, what in tarnation were you thinking of? Don't you realize you had us all worried? An' you, Jason, shooting up my foreman and putting another of my men out of action. D'you both think I haven't worries enough?'

'I figure,' Jason began evenly, 'that you've got the branding-iron out afore you've roped the steer.'

'What the hell's that s'posed to mean?' Zeb roared, drawing his lips back in a snarl.

Jason cupped his hands around his glass and savoured the good liquor, feeling an anger building up inside him.

'It means that you've bin the cause of most of the trouble that's bin brewing. I came to this town peaceful. Twice I've bin shot at by you and twice I've bin told it'd be better fer my health if I high-tailed it outa here. An' once I've seen the inside of a cell. It sticks in my craw that a man can't mind his own business without being hounded.'

Zeb took a deep breath, then let it out again as Carter Brown rounded on him. He leaned back in his chair with a growl.

'Enough! I'll not tolerate more of that. Remember, both of you, that my daughter's in this room and doesn't want to listen to two men brawling.'

'Thanks, Pa,' Grace said. 'But I've heard it all before.'

'No reason why you should listen to it from guests in my house.' He glared at the two men. 'This has to stop. Zeb, I expect you to apologize to Jason. This whole thing has gone too far. I want it to end.'

But Zeb was having none of it. 'You're goddamnn right, it's gone too far. Too far to back out. I should've nailed him the first time I set eyes on him.'

Jason wondered at the aggression the man was showing. There were undertones here that he couldn't get a grip on.

'I don't need no apology, Mr Brown,'

he said. 'I need a job, that's all. An' like I said, I'll be happy to work under Zeb's instructions long as they're fair an' reasonable.'

Carter Brown looked from one to the other. There was a tension in his eyes. 'Right. That's how it'll be, then. Zeb, I wanna talk to you in private so perhaps you, Grace, will take Jason up to see the sheriff if the doc's finished with him. When I've spoken to Zeb you and me are going to have a long talk.'

'OK. Pa,' Grace said wearily.

Jason drained his glass and stood up as he waited for Grace to do as her pa had asked. Zeb's eyes followed his every movement and what Jason saw in them gave him no reason to believe that this was to be the end of the matter.

He followed Grace along a carpeted hallway lined with framed pictures and up a short flight of stairs. She indicated a door on the right of the passage from which came the sound of the sheriff's voice angrily calling for his pants.

'He sounds a mite riled,' Jason said.

'I think he'll be more friendly if I can take him his clothes.'

'Wait there.' She went into another room and emerged with the sheriff's pants, and leather vest. She also handed Jason the sheriff's gunbelt.

Jason thanked her and knocked, entering without waiting for a reply. He could hardly keep the smile from his face. Kelly Quintock, in his long johns and undershirt, was sitting on the edge of his bed. A bandage covered the top of his head.

'About time,' he growled when he saw what Jason was carrying. 'It ain't right fer a man to be kept without his pants and gun. Makes him kinda handicapped. Unless of course,' he added with a grin, 'he's got other interests.'

'Reckoned you might be pleased to see me,' Jason said.

The sheriff donned his pants and buckled on his gunbelt. He checked his pistol and slipped it back into its holster. 'Yeah, you could say that. You saved my hide. I guess I owe you my life.' He pushed his feet into his boots and stood up.

'I picked you outa the dust, is all.'

'I'm obliged. But you should've bin in jail. Who let you out?'

'Your deputy was kind enough. And Carter Brown.'

The sheriff raised his eyebrows. 'I wonder why he did that? Anyways, I'm sorta glad they did.'

'You owe me an explanation,' Jason said. 'I wanna know what's going on. Who shot you? You an' Grace were both bein' chased. What in tarnation were you doing so far out? Wasn't that outside yer jurisdiction?'

'Yeah, sure, but I was trailing that young bank robber, Billy Manning, hoping he'd lead me to the hideout.'

'And? Where did he go?'

The sheriff grimaced. 'He gave me the slip. He's either more cunning than I figured or I'm getting too old for the job.'

'Where do I fit in? I get the impression I'm a key figure in all this an' I don't know what part I'm s'posed to play.'

'Whoa. You're givin' me a headache. That's too many questions for a man with a sore head to answer. But I'll tell you what I do know if'n you'll be good enough to do the same. There's something goin' on round here but I haven't got a bead on it yet. I don't know whether you're involved or not.'

'Sheriff, I came to this town mindin' my own business. Seems to me I was doin' my civic duty in stopping yer bank from bein' robbed but now I'm being sucked into something an' I'm a mite sick on it.'

The sheriff gave him a long stare. 'I'm a good judge of men and I think I can trust you, you bein' a stranger and mebbe not taken sides yet.'

'Sounds like you're gonna suck me in still further. Not sure I like the sound o' that.'

'If you stick around you gonna have to take one side or the other. I'll level with you. I aim to nail that outlaw you seemed so all-fired interested in back at the jail.'

'Adam One-ear?'

'Yeah. So the story goes he returned home after the war to find his family had bin killed by a band of Bluebelly guerrillas. But that don't excuse him from goin' bad.'

'So, you're out to get him?'

'Yeah, and his gang o' cut-throats. The Redford gang, hardcases, all o' them. They've caused mayhem in this neck of the woods fer long enough.'

'And there's five thousand dollars on his head?'

The sheriff grinned. 'That as well.'

'It's a big motive.'

'I don't mind tellin' you that reward is gonna be my retirement fund. I aim to hand in my badge and enjoy the rest of my days. Have you got yer eyes on the reward? If you have, you'd best come clean now.'

'Nope, Sheriff, and you can take that as gospel.'

'Just as well. Wouldn't do you no

good. What's your interest, then?'

Jason's mind recalled the hell of the war he had been through. 'The man you call Adam One-ear may have saved my life, Sheriff. I never had a chance to say thanks. He had no need to do what he did since we were fighting each other at the time.'

'Hmm.' The sheriff was thoughtful. 'You won't mind if I shoot him once you've said your piece?'

'Can't rightly say,' Jason said. 'Don't know till I see him.'

'I had in mind to ask you to help me find the varmint. What d'ya say?'

'Since you'll be out o' yer bailiwick, you won't be able to deputize me, will you?'

'Well, you're right there, Jason. But this has nothin' to do with my badge. I'll admit it has everythin' to do with money.'

'You'll need a posse, I reckon. Even then it won't be easy.'

'Two's the right number. You an' me. Are you on?'

'I'll give it some thought,' Jason said. He felt weary from a long day in the saddle and lack of good food.

He left the room and wandered downstairs, chewing over the sheriff's proposal. As he passed the door to the room he had recently been in he heard the rancher's voice raised in anger and the harsher tones of Zeb in reply. He left them to it.

The sky was dark outside, studded with stars, although clouds were building up. A freshening breeze cooled the air and he stood on the porch breathing in the familiar scents and odours of a busy ranch.

Could two men achieve what a posse could not? He knew the large reward would have invited any number of bounty hunters to capture or kill the outlaw. The fact that they had not succeeded was evidence that Adam One-ear would not be an easy target.

He shrugged. He'd just reached a decision when he saw Lew walking across the yard towards the bunkhouse.

He hurried over and grasped the old man's shoulder.

'I need to know what's going on here,' he said. 'You gave me a warning and told me a man had disappeared. How could he just disappear? Am I s'posed to disappear?'

Lew still seemed reluctant to talk but Jason was encouraged when he didn't immediately pull away.

'Can't speak here,' Lew said and led Jason over to the barn. He stopped inside the door where the shadow was deep. 'Not much I can tell you. I have suspicions. A drifter like you came looking fer work. I believe he was the spittin' image of a local outlaw who had a price on his head, dead or alive.

'Shortly after that the drifter just vanished. So did the outlaw. And Zeb claimed the reward. Said he'd killed the outlaw and had the dead body to prove it. That's all I know but I've bin around a long time an' I kin smell a rat without seein' it.'

Jason retained his hold on Lew's arm

while he took in what he was being told. 'You're tellin' me that Zeb substituted a dead body for a wanted outlaw, then claimed the reward? Can't believe it'd work out. Anyway, what's that gotta do with me?'

Lew tried to pull away. 'I've already said too much.'

'You haven't told me anywhere near enough. What else d'ya know? What else is Zeb involved in?'

'I'm not one to be shootin' off my mouth,' Lew snarled. 'I'm paid to do a job an' I do it an' that doesn't include tellin' tales.'

Jason increased his grip. 'I don't cotton to mysteries, specially when my life's involved. Tell me what you know or I'll break your arm.' He twisted hard and, although he had no intention of carrying out his threat, he was pleased to see that Lew thought he would. 'What else is goin' on?'

'OK. No cause to git rough. I b'lieve Zeb has connections with the outlaws. Helps them to rustle the CB cattle. I heard him talkin' once to Duke. They meet at a shack about a day an' a half's ride from here. That's all I know.'

'Have you told any of this to Carter Brown?'

Lew shook his head vigorously. 'Not my business.'

Jason studied him. 'Well, it's sure as hell my business,' he said and released his hold. Lew turned without another word and walked away.

Jason stayed where he was in deep thought for several minutes, then he went back inside to talk again with the sheriff.

8

Zeb had waited until Jason and Grace left the room to see the sheriff before he leapt to his feet and confronted his half-brother, his eyes conveying the venom he felt.

'What in hell d'ya think you're doing?' he bellowed. 'Are you forgettin' what we want that drifter for?'

Carter Brown was taken aback by the fury of the attack. 'We'd agreed to call an end to this nonsense!'

Zeb went to the cabinet and refilled his glass. 'We'd agreed nothing,' he said. 'Except perhaps that since your pa left you this ranch an' I was left nothin' you've allowed it to lose money until now you owe the bank almost as much as it's worth.'

'Every rancher has to borrow now and again,' Carter protested. 'You know we've had difficulties. Everyone around these parts has had problems with the rain bein' short these past two years. Now we've got a prime herd almost ready to go. They'll bring in more'n enough to wipe out the debt.'

'You're losin' steers every day. What're you doin' about that?'

'That's your job, Zeb. You're the foreman but you seem to have your mind on other things.'

Zeb downed his second glass of liquor and returned to the cabinet for more. 'It's as well one of us remembers what we'd planned. It worked fer us before. This time it'll bring in five thousand dollars. Just think on it. You'd need to sell a heap o' cows to make that.' He cupped his hands around the glass.

Carter Brown shook his head. 'Zeb, before was different. The outlaw came to us and was more'n happy to do what we suggested. He wanted the heat taken off. All we did was to dress up the dead man to look like him. He got what he wanted and so did we. We were fortunate then to have a friendly judge to issue the certificate. He owed us a favour. We've not got that advantage this time. Anyway,' Carter Brown added, 'the drifter was dead. We didn't kill him so no real crime was committed.'

Zeb's laughter came from his belly but it was without mirth. 'The drifter was already dead? What d'ya reckon killed him? Old age? He died, sure, but more like from lead poisoning.'

For the space of half a minute the rancher considered what Zeb was telling him, incomprehension giving way to shock.

'You shot him!'

'You've known that all along,' Zeb said. 'Jest didn't want to think on it. Left me to do the dirty work while you netted the reward. Two thousand dollars that time. Now it's more'n double that. You're in this too deep to get out.'

The rancher raised his voice. 'I'm not doing it, Zeb. Neither are you. It's over.

We're not killing a man in cold blood.'

'Mebbe you can't. I can. Specially a varmint like Jason Flowers. You invited him into your home. Well, he won't be coming here a second time.'

'Every man makes a mistake once in a while,' Carter Brown breathed. 'And I've made too many. I'm not making any more.'

'Jason Flowers is worth a lotta money to us.'

'Not to me or to you. You're not doing it. Let's be thankful that we got away with it once, but never again! I'll not have it.'

'You've no choice. He'd be dead now if Duke hadda bin less handy on the trigger.'

'Way I heard it Jason had the drop on you both.'

'We could've taken him. Now we have him right here it'd be easy as ropin' a crippled steer. We'll cut off his ear and mess his face up a mite.'

'You're right on one thing, Zeb, this is my home and Jason Flowers is a guest here. He brought my daughter back safe an' I owe him. He stays unharmed.'

There was poison in Zeb's voice. 'It's gonna happen.'

'We'll see. How d'you know Adam One-ear wants to go along with this?'

'Ain't it obvious? I've bin talking to the man.'

'How the hell did you manage that?'

A self-satisfied look appeared on Zeb's sullen features. 'You an' me, though you mebbe didn't know it, we've bin givin' him shelter. In that ol' shack. Bin unoccupied for nigh on four years. Served Adam well when he was bein' chased. And, with five thousand dollars on his head, he knows it's just a matter o' time before some varmint gets lucky. He'd appreciate not havin' bounty hunters and the law on his trail all the time, so the sooner we can say we've killed him and claim the reward the happier he'll be. An' we'll be richer,' he added.

'Get out!' Carter Brown yelled. 'Get

out of my house before I have you thrown off this ranch. You've no claim here. You have a job here because Ma requested it, but what I say goes. Just remember that.'

'Well, mebbe you won't be around fer too long.' Zeb shut off abruptly as if he'd said too much.

'You'd best make yourself plain,' Carter Brown snapped. 'If that's the way you feel go find somewhere else to work. I'll tell you this. The law's gonna know what's been going on and the law can deal with it.'

'You think you control the law around these parts? Mebbe you used to but not any longer. I've got more influence than you ever had.' Zeb appeared as if he intended to continue the argument, then he shrugged. 'So that's how it is. We started this and I mean to finish it.'

The rancher's face turned white with fury. 'I'll have no truck with the local law. I'll get a federal marshal down.'

'You'll do no such thing. You're in

this as much as I am.'

'It doesn't matter any more. I was weak. That's the end of the matter. Get out now before I have you kicked out.' Then, as Zeb's hand hovered over his Colt, Carter Brown said, 'You reckon on killing me? Go ahead. You'll be hunted like the coyote you are.'

Zeb strutted to the door and flung it open. 'I'll save that pleasure fer later.' As he went through and slammed the door shut behind him he collided with Grace, sending her stumbling against the far wall. He stared at her for a moment, then hissed, 'You bin listenin'?'

She pushed herself back on to her feet. 'None of your business.'

'Oh, but it is my business. What did you hear?'

'I heard enough!' Her eyes flamed. 'Now, I want to talk to Pa. Get outa my way.'

Instead of moving aside he put his face close to hers. 'Whatever you heard is no business of yours. Unnerstand?

It's between your pa an' me. You stay out of it.'

She shoved him aside and he reluctantly gave way but not before he'd given her a spiteful glare that made her catch her breath. After the door had shut he remained outside, his mind working, weighing up the options available to him. He was determined that his half-brother was not going to spoil his plans, but he was certain that if the law became involved there would be hell to pay.

Gradually an idea entered his head and the more he thought about it the wider his grin grew. He left the building as the wind gained in strength and storm clouds gathered. The worsening weather matched his mood.

When he returned he could hear Grace and her pa still talking in the room he had recently left. He was patient, knowing that he couldn't rush what he was about to do and that he would have only one chance to carry it off. He hid in the doorway of a nearby room.

When Grace emerged her shoulders were hunched as if a great weight sat on them. She looked straight ahead, obviously lost in thought. That suited Zeb. As she passed him he lunged, placed a bag over her head, wrapped one powerful arm around her body and a placed a large hand over her mouth. She struggled and a scream, muffled by the cover, was stifled almost before it began.

'No noise,' he growled. 'Or you get a slug in the guts.' He knew he couldn't do that because the sound of a shot in the building would bring people running. But he aimed to scare her and was fully prepared to bring the butt of his Colt sharply to the side of her head to avoid detection. Nevertheless she struggled. Her flailing feet caught Zeb painfully on his shins and her wild movements sent agonizing pains down his injured arm.

'Goddamn it. Stay still,' he growled.

Grace was stronger than he thought and in the end he was forced to use his gun to keep her quiet. She slumped and he hoped he hadn't overdone it.

He lifted her off her feet, carried her outside to where he had left Duke with orders to get the horses saddled up and ready. Duke was waiting, as he had been instructed. Also patiently cropping the grass was Grace's pinto, an integral part of Zeb's plan.

'Help me tie her up,' he said.

They removed the cover from her head and gagged her, then bound her hands before replacing the bag. Zeb checked that she was still breathing before they heaved her on to her horse, tied her hands to the pommel and looped a rope around her neck, the other end of which Zeb secured to his own horse. Grace was still groggy from the blow on the head and was in danger of sliding off.

'Careful,' Zeb hissed. 'We don't wanna kill her just yet.' When she seemed steady he grunted with satisfaction.

They mounted their own horses and

as silently as possible left the ranch and headed down the trail, Zeb leading.

'As easy as takin' a hoss to water,' Zeb said. 'A day an' a half's ride an' we're done.' As far as he was aware nobody had seen them leave.

'They'll follow,' Duke said. 'Won't take 'em long to catch us up.'

Zeb grinned. 'It's gonna rain afore long. Fat chance they'll have of findin' our tracks after that.'

They followed the same route as the sheriff and Grace had taken the previous day. Zeb knew exactly where they were heading because he had been there many times before. He felt sure of a friendly welcome at the hideout.

He was right about the weather. By the time they had travelled for two hours ominous clouds were rushing across the heavens, bringing with them shafts of rain that soaked into their clothes and ran down the flanks of their horses. The ground quickly turned to mud. Their clothes dragged at their limbs and rain seeped down their necks.

Grace soon recovered consciousness and attempted to remove the mask, finding breathing difficult through the wet cloth covering her face. Zeb leaned over and removed the bag for her.

'How d'ya feel?' he asked.

'No better for seeing your ugly face.' She spat out the words and took in large gulps of air. Her body ached and she felt strangely light-headed. Tiredness dragged at her eyelids.

They pulled their horses in at a small creek, dismounted, and sheltered as best they could, although they had no hope of lighting a fire.

'We've made a good start but we'll have to push on,' Zeb said, hunching down against the chill. 'It's a long ride but we kin brew up some coffee later on an' mebbe fill our bellies at the shack.'

'How am I s'posed to drink, trussed up like a chicken? My head hurts. What're you gonna do about that?'

'Can't do nothin' about it. It's your fault fer fightin' me. Now, I'm gonna untie yer hands but don't get any ideas

141

about escaping.' He handed her some hardtack biscuits to chew on. He kept hold of the rope around her neck. 'Try anythin' an' you'll be trussed up again.'

'Why're you doing this? You know this is a kidnapping offence. You'll be facing the rope.'

'No chance o' that.'

'You know what Pa'll do when he finds out.'

Zeb grinned. 'Yeah, I know. He'll do just what I tell him to do.'

'Goddamn it! Where're you taking me?'

Zeb gave a tight grin. 'Swearin' don't suit young ladies.'

Grace struggled to free herself from the rope. 'I'm no lady. An' if you let me go I'll show you!'

'Can't do that.'

'I asked you where you're taking me.'

'So you did. Well, I'll tell ya. You're gonna be the guest of a very fine outlaw. He's rather fond of women, is Adam One-ear.'

This came as a surprise. 'Adam One-ear!'

'Yep, but don't call him that to his face if you wanna keep on living.'

Grace was silent after that and Zeb left her to digest the information.

Out of earshot Duke asked, 'She's ya brother's daughter, Zeb. What's this all about?'

'Let me do the thinkin', Duke. But, yeah, she's my half-brother's daughter an' I've no love for either of 'em. The sooner they go to meet their Maker the better. I'll take control of the ranch then an' I'll make a better job of it than Carter has. If he goes to the authorities with his story there'll be the law swarming all over the place an' I'll have lost my chance. Once he realizes his daughter's life's at stake he'll think twice.

'Now, keep a lookout,' he instructed, though he didn't expect anyone to be following immediately.

He reasoned that Grace's pa would think she had ridden off somewhere to be on her own. When they realized she hadn't and decided to do something about it they would be a long way behind.

With the rain showing no signs of easing they pushed on although the going was slow. They intended to put as much distance between themselves and any possible pursuers as quickly as possible. Grace found herself dozing in the saddle.

Eventually they were relieved to see the morning sun which, swiftly building up heat, soon dried their clothes and drew the moisture from the ground, hardening the adobe soil.

9

Although Zeb thought no one had noticed him leave he was wrong. One of the hands who had gone outside for a smoke before turning in for the night had spotted him. He had done nothing about it. It had been a hard day, and if someone wanted to continue working it was no concern of his.

Meanwhile, following his talk with Lew, Jason conveyed what he had learned to Kelly Quintock. Kelly listened intently, his brow furrowed in deep thought.

'That's it,' Jason said. 'It's not much to go on but when you consider the warnings I've had, the fact that Zeb clearly wanted me dead, and Carter Brown's offer of work to me as a complete stranger, it all seems to add up.'

'But add up to what?' the sheriff

asked. 'What I'm thinkin' don't make sense. I've known Carter Brown fer a number of years an' if I was asked I'd say this is more Zeb's style than his.'

'And what about Grace? Where does she fit in?'

'My guess is that she suspects but doesn't really know. Anyways,' he added with a smile, 'you seem to know her better than I do.'

'I reckon,' Jason agreed. 'I think I'll go an' talk with her some more.'

Carter Brown met them in the passage. His brow was furrowed. 'Seen my daughter?' he asked. 'I was talking to her an hour or so ago and now she's missing again. She was upset an' she may've gone off somewhere.'

'What was on her mind?' Jason asked. 'She was fine when I brought her in.'

'Personal.' The rancher's words were clipped. 'Have you seen her?'

Jason shook his head. 'Would she have gone off on her own in the dark?'

'She's never bin so angry before.'

'Her horse is missing?'

'Yep. So is Zeb's. Tom's just told me.' Carter Brown indicated the hand who had brought the news. 'Should've told me sooner.' His eyes blazed.

Jason felt the hairs on his neck rise. 'She wouldn't've gone willingly with Zeb.'

'It's possible Grace just wanted a place to think an' has taken off somewhere quiet,' the sheriff offered, although it was clear from his eyes that he wasn't convinced.

'No.' The rancher visibly paled. 'Zeb's taken her to keep me quiet. I can't believe he'd do such a thing.'

Jason's jaw tightened. 'Or for a ransom,' he suggested. 'Any notion which way they might've gone?' he asked.

The hand nodded. 'Too dark to make out much but there're tracks leading out. They look fresh but it's difficult to tell. I heard Zeb an' Duke talkin' about restin' over in a shack somewhere. I didn't know there was no one with 'em.'

147

Jason turned to the sheriff. 'Fit to ride?'

'Take more'n a clip on the head to put me out o' action,' he said. 'Might even have knocked some sense into me. What's on yer mind? Can't do much till sunup.'

'Sooner we act the better. If we're right we can't wait fer daylight an' if we're wrong we'll've just had a ride fer nothing.' He thought for a moment, then asked the rancher, 'Is there one o' the hands knows the country well enough who might know for sure where they could've bin headed? The tracks may give us a lead of direction.'

'Bring Lew here,' he told Tom. 'If anyone knows he will.'

Lew turned out to be more than willing. He'd been working at the ranch when Grace had been born and had done his best to look after her interests from that day on.

'There's that shack, few miles off the main trail up beyond Red Canyon,' he told them. 'Seen Zeb headin' in that

148

direction a few times.'

'D'ya reckon?'

'It's outa the way. Few people know about it. Good place to hide out,' Lew said. 'Take you a day and a half's ridin' to get there.'

The sheriff slapped his thigh. 'That's where that young varmint was headin' when I got shot,' he said. 'I reckon that's where the shooters came from.'

'You think they might be usin' the shack?'

'Yep. I was sure he was makin' fer the Redford gang. An' I guess that the shooters were members of the gang an' they didn't want me around. Or else . . . ' a thought occurred to him, 'or else that young snake intended to fill me with lead all the time I was trailin' him.'

'And,' Carter Brown intervened, 'Zeb told me he'd made contact with the gang on at least two occasions.'

'That settles it,' Jason said. 'They either use the shack as a hideout or more likely as an occasional place to

stay while they're robbin' an' mur-
derin'.'

'Either way,' Kelly Quintock said.
'It's time we paid 'em a visit.'

Carter Brown was more cautious.
'Look at the weather,' he warned. 'It's
no use setting off now. We don't know
fer sure what's happened. Grace could
turn up at any time. An' if she doesn't
it's best if you wait till sunup and the
weather's cleared. You'll make better
time then. On a full belly,' he added.

Jason was reluctant to agree. All his
instincts screamed at him to set off in
hot pursuit but he saw the wisdom of
what Carter Brown was saying. He was
tired and hungry and, if he set off on
the trail again, would need to keep
alert.

'Will you need more men?' the
rancher asked.

'Nope,' Jason said. 'Two of us stand a
better chance of sneaking up on them.
Once we get close Lew can double
back. If we don't return in three days
you can send as many men as you like.'

'Right.' Carter Brown seemed to reach a decision. 'I invited you to dinner an' the food's spoiling.' He led Jason and the sheriff towards the dining room where a large, highly polished table was set with four places and bowls of fruit and bread. The window, stretching from floor to ceiling, looked out on to the yard and the trees beyond. Leaves rattled on the glass, blown there by the strengthening wind.

They sat in silence, each eyeing the vacant place where Grace should have been. Food was brought to them, steaming dishes with appetizing aromas. But only the sheriff did justice to the meal.

'I don't like waiting,' Jason said, voicing the thoughts of the other two.

'Neither do I,' Carter said. 'But it's for the best. It's too dark out. Get some rest, then an early breakfast. You'll make good time after that.'

By the time they had finished eating rain beat on the window like bullets.

The men went to their beds. Despite his misgivings Jason was soon asleep.

* * *

Despite lack of sleep and an empty belly Grace sat upright in the saddle, determined not to let her captors see she was scared. For scared she was.

She was in the hands of two men who, if not her friends, had not been her enemies until now. Not only that, her head hurt where Zeb had hit her, she was hungry and her throat was so dry as to make swallowing difficult. Her hands were securely tied to the pommel.

As she rode her pinto alongside Zeb she knew she was in serious trouble and the attitude of the two men gave her no confidence for her immediate future.

She sucked in deep breaths of the early morning air. 'Why're you doing this?'

'Don't mean you no harm, Grace,' Zeb said. 'But we gotta bring your pa to heel.'

'You know he'll send men looking for me,' she said.

'Yeah,' Zeb growled. 'They kin look all they want but they won't find you till I'm ready.'

'Where're you taking me?'

'I've told ya,' Zeb said. 'You'll be the guest of my friend, Adam. Only a while till yer pa sees sense.'

Grace considered this. 'But when you go back to the ranch Pa'll know what you've done.'

Zeb grinned, self-satisfaction evident on his face. 'That's the clever part of my plan. 'Sfar as they'll know I'll be a hero. I chased after the outlaws that took you. Pity I didn't manage to rescue you, of course.' He chuckled.

Grace gasped at the implication. 'An' what about Duke? Why's he in on this crazy scheme?'

Zeb gave no reply and Grace, sensing a weakness, continued. 'Does he know what you have in mind for him?'

Zeb screwed round in the saddle. 'If ya don't shut yer mouth I'll put the bag

153

over yer head agin.'

Grace wasn't to be put off. She glanced back at Duke. Maybe he was to be expendable. That was certainly to be her fate.

'Best thing you can do, Zeb,' she began, 'is to turn round and head for home.'

'I told ya what I'd do if you didn't shut up.' He urged his horse forward.

'OK,' Grace eased her own mount, allowing Duke to draw level.

They rode side by side for a while in silence. She looked across at the man who had said hardly a word to her from the beginning. His expression did not encourage conversation. At last she said, 'What harm have I done to you, Duke? I thought you enjoyed working at Pa's ranch.'

Duke glanced sideways. At first Grace thought he was not going to answer, then he said, 'It won't be yer pa's much longer.'

He sounded so sure that she felt a shiver of fear down her spine. 'What're you talking about? It'll always be Pa's an' then maybe mine one day. Never Zeb's.'

A snarl creased Duke's mouth. 'You're here, ain't ya? Zeb's got plans. He knows what he's doin'. Him an' me, we're pards.'

'Like makin' friends with a coyote,' Grace said, hoping to encourage him to say more.

Zeb turned. 'What in tarnation are you two gabbin' about? If you open ya mouth again . . . '

Grace urged her horse forward. 'All right, Zeb. I gotta talk to someone and you clammed up on me.'

'Save ya breath. We're nearly there.'

It had been a hot and tiring journey. The sun was at its highest. Ahead Grace saw how the trail wound across the rocky ground towards a small log cabin set back against the face of a bluff. A small creek nearby ran between stands of sycamore and willow.

'Old prospector's shack,' Zeb said. 'Not many people know it's here.'

As they drew nearer Grace noticed that the vegetation around the shack had been beaten flat as if by both men and horses.

Zeb called a halt while they were several hundred yards away and, from a rise, he surveyed the area.

'Don't see no one,' he observed. 'Great. Should be food and drink there an' a coupla beds.' He grinned at Grace. 'This is where we rest awhile. Hope ya cookin's good.'

He led the way to the shack and approached it openly. 'If there is someone there we don't want 'em to think we mean trouble. Anyways, they should recognize me afore they start shooting.' He laughed at his own joke but neither Grace or Duke joined in.

They dismounted and entered through the wooden door, Zeb giving Grace a heavy-handed push that sent her reeling to her knees. The shack was indeed unoccupied, although there were signs indicating that people had been both eating and sleeping there.

Two beds were set against the walls, food and coffee were stacked in makeshift cupboards. A table and chairs stood in the centre of the small room while a black iron stove gave promise of hot meals.

'Get the stove going,' Zeb said to Duke. 'Then see to the horses. Loosen the cinches. We ain't stoppin' long. There's hay out back an' a trough. Make sure they're secure.' He stood and looked around at the few comforts that the shack offered. 'This sure is goin' to be cosy.'

Grace dragged herself to her feet. With her hands still bound there was little she could do to defend herself against anything they had in mind for her. 'How about untying me,' she said. 'I can't cook like this.'

'All in good time.' Zeb pointed to the bucket standing empty near the stove. 'First you kin make yerself useful. We'll need some water from the creek an' then you kin bring in some wood. After that we'll see how good yer cookin' is.'

Grace showed her anger. 'I'll do nothing till you take these ropes off.'

'Suit yerself,' Zeb growled. 'Then you get nothing to eat.' He left the bindings securing her hands.

She picked up the bucket and went outside. Given free access to her horse, she could probably outrun any pursuit but, bound as she was and on foot, a bullet in the back would quickly put an end to her freedom.

Within half an hour there was a pot heating on the stove with the odour of corn mash and beef filling the cabin. Zeb had found some whiskey stashed in a corner and he helped himself generously. Duke did the same but Grace would have none of it. The atmosphere within the room was thick with the strong smell of liquor and cooking.

'Later,' Zeb announced, his words slurring a little, 'we'll be pushin' on soon enough.' He eyed the two beds. 'Meantime I reckon it's time for a bit o' fun.' His gaze shifted to Grace.

'Not with me, you're not!' she fired back at him. There was no doubt in her mind what Zeb intended to do and she was determined that, if he tried, it would be the last thing he ever did.

He shuffled over to her and there was little space for her to avoid his advance. She backed away until she was hard up against the shelf containing the cooking pans.

He grabbed her arm and she struggled to release his grasping fingers. 'You can't do this,' she yelled. 'You're my uncle!'

Zeb grinned savagely. 'Not by my reckonin' I'm not.'

But she realized no words were going to be sufficient to hold him off. She felt along the shelf and her fingers curled round the handle of a cast-iron cooking-pot.

Zeb turned round to Duke. 'You go an' scout around fer a while,' he said. 'Take yer time.'

Grace took the opportunity and swept the pot hard towards the back of

Zeb's head. But the pot was heavy and the noise of it scraping along the shelf alerted him. He whirled back, receiving the blow on his wounded shoulder. With a grunt of pain and anger he swung his fist, catching Grace on the side of her jaw. She collapsed without a sound.

'Dammit to hell,' Zeb growled. 'What fer did the silly bitch do that?'

Grace wasn't moving. Zeb bent over her. He lifted her roughly and laid her out on the floor. 'Won't be no good to us if she's dead,' he said. 'Not fer now, anyways.' He poured himself some coffee.

10

Despite his weariness of the night before Jason woke early and roused the sheriff. The storm had abated and, although the sun had not yet risen, the air was still and the sky gave promise of another clear day. They drank coffee, checked their weapons and packed provisions for the journey. Carter Brown appeared as if he had been up all night and was issuing urgent instructions to all the staff.

'I'm sending out more search teams,' he said. Then he turned his gaze on Jason and the sheriff. 'Bring her back to me.'

'If she's where we think she is you can bet yer bottom dollar on it,' Jason promised, knowing in his mind that it might not be as simple as that.

The soft moon, looking like a slice of melon, was fading as dawn approached and Lew led Jason and the sheriff from the ranch.

They rode throughout the day with occasional rests to refresh the horses and to stretch their limbs. The going was heavy until the hot sun dried the ground but they pushed on as hard as they could without wasting their mounts. They were relying on Lew to take them in the right direction because any hope of seeing tracks had vanished with the heavy rain.

Night came again with a blaze of red and orange over the distant mountains, to find them still in the saddle. They had made good progress.

'Best rest up a while,' Jason suggested. He was tense, eager to press on, but recognized the wisdom of remaining fresh for the remainder of the journey.

They camped by a quick-running rill. They made coffee and heated their food over a small fire. The horses drank eagerly from the cool water.

'How much further?' Jason asked.

'We must be catching up with them.'

'Should be there a little after noon,' Lew told him. 'Depends how long we stay here.'

'Coupla hours' sleep or so should see us all right,' Jason said. 'We need a full belly and the horses need a break.' The smell of frying bacon wafted across to him and he realized how long it was since they had eaten with any pleasure.

He turned to the sheriff. 'You let Billy out o' jail so's you could follow him. But when you found the hideout, what then?'

'Hadn't thought that far ahead,' the sheriff admitted. 'But I never got near it. The varmint must've seen me on his trail,' he added ruefully, clearly dismayed at his trailing skills. 'Must be gettin' old.'

'What would you've done? On yer own against who knows how many?'

'Mebbe high-tailed it back an' rounded up a posse.'

'Where d'ya reckon Billy fits in to all this?'

The sheriff scratched his chin. 'He's a young man with a grudge. He's lookin' fer revenge. There's no tellin' where that'll lead him. At the moment he seems to have fallen in with Adam One-ear. That won't do him no good either.'

'Do we know how many outlaws are in the gang?'

'It's a small band, so I've heard tell. No more'n six or seven last I heard. But they're hard-nosed scum, all of 'em.'

'Well, I just hope the two of us'll be able to rescue Grace before they get their hands on her. Zeb's gotta lot to answer for.'

Lew had been listening to the two men. 'Three of us,' he said. 'I ain't about to be left outa this.'

'No,' Jason said at once. 'I know you kin handle a firearm, Lew, but you're not a gunfighter. The two of us can handle them varmints an' I don't want to be worryin' about you.' Realizing he had been too hard he added, 'Any case, once we know where Grace is being

164

held it'd be best fer you to high-tail it back an' let the others know.'

Lew nodded but clearly he was upset.

They finished their supper, then rolled into their blankets and slept. The night sky was clear, the stars filling the heavens, and the water of the rill sang over the stones.

Jason woke first, brought the fire to life and heated some coffee before he roused the others. The only light came from the moon but that was enough and they set about preparing for their departure.

They mounted up and rode on in silence, watching for the pink light of dawn to show itself in the east. They rode through the heat of the morning until Lew said, 'We're gettin' close. Over that rise an' we'll be able to see the shack.'

They automatically checked their weapons and, proceeding cautiously, turned off the trail and dismounted at the top of a small rise about half a mile away. They ground-hitched their mounts and edged forward, then bellied down, peering over the edge, from where they had a clear view of the area. Smoke was curling lazily from the roof of the small building but there was no sign of any activity outside.

'Don't seem to be expecting trouble,' Jason observed.

'Wonder how many are there?' Kelly mused. 'Only seem to be three hosses out back.'

Jason took the glasses from his saddle-bag and swept the scene below him. 'Yep,' he said with rising excitement, 'And one of them's Grace's pinto. She's in there, an' probably two others.'

'Zeb an' Duke,' the sheriff growled.

As they watched a man came out of the shack and paused in the doorway to light a cigar. He gazed around but his stance was casual and relaxed and he clearly saw nothing to alarm him.

After a minute or so he walked round to the corralled area towards the rear of the building and began to tighten the cinches of the horses.

'Looks like they're goin' somewhere,' Jason said. 'Don't seem to be in too much of a hurry, though.' He peered through the glasses. 'It's Zeb. Duke must still be inside.' He turned to Lew. 'You've done a good job,' he told him. 'Time fer you to vamoose.'

Lew slid back from the rise, mounted and wheeled his horse as he reluctantly set off back the way they had come.

'What's our plan?' Kelly asked. 'Tackle 'em head on?'

Jason gave it some thought. 'No knowing what they'd do. We don't want a gun battle if we can avoid it.'

This met with Kelly's approval. 'I guess our first call will be to get Grace outa there safely. Though I'd like to follow Zeb if he's going to the hideout.'

'We'll get round to Adam later,' Jason said. He studied the layout. 'We can't approach from the back. If you go on foot you kin angle round to the side without being seen an' wait in that shallow draw till I reach the stand o'

167

trees facing the front. OK?'

'I'll wait fer ya signal.' He cradled his Winchester, checked his six-gun again and left, crouching low. Jason watched him, then set off for the trees by a more circular route.

By the time he was in position Zeb had brought the horses round to the front and hitched them by the door. He was clearly not expecting trouble and stood easy, enjoying the warmth while he finished his cigar.

'I'm gonna wipe that self-satisfied look off yer face,' Jason muttered.

He took a breath and was about to call out when the muted clatter of horses' hoofs reached his ears. Two riders, he reckoned, approaching at an easy pace, and he waited for them to come into view. Along the trail that led away from the shack the riders appeared.

As they drew closer he recognized the men as those he had shot earlier and was mildly surprised to see them still in the saddle after the injuries he and

Grace had inflicted on them. He waited.

'Howdy, Zeb,' the larger of the two men called in a voice loud enough for Jason to hear. 'What in tarnation you doin' here?' It did not surprise Jason that he and Zeb were well acquainted.

By way of reply Zeb went back into the shack, then came out dragging Grace by the arm. Zeb spoke but his voice was low. It was not difficult, however, for Jason to fit words to the actions.

The big man did not appear pleased. 'What the hell have you brought her along fer? This ain't no place fer a woman.'

Zeb said something else that brought a roar of laughter in response. 'Yer best git goin' then. Adam seems to be takin' on all sorts just lately.'

The men slid off the backs of their horses. 'We're stayin' here fer a while,' the smaller of the two said. His voice was high-pitched and carried easily. 'We've bin told to clear out the shack.

169

We won't be usin' it no more. Seems Adam's got another place in mind.'

He peered closely at Grace. 'Not bad lookin' when you haven't been with a woman fer a while. Reckon you've done well. We'll take care o' her if you like.' He laughed again.

Jason would have liked Duke to show himself so all the men were in sight but he knew he had to act before the hardcases went into the shack. He hoped the sheriff had sight of what was going on from where he was concealed.

He took another breath. 'Keep yer hands where I kin see them,' he shouted. 'I only wanna talk.'

His command had the opposite effect to what he wanted and he knew immediately that he should have allowed for the instinctive reactions of experienced gunnies. The two men, without a moment's hesitation threw themselves sideways, one to the left and the other to the right, seeking what cover they could find and drawing their weapons with practised skill.

Zeb seemed momentarily paralysed, but swiftly recovered and pulled Grace in front of him for protection as he backed through the door of the shack.

'Damn,' Jason muttered as a fusillade of shots was sent in his direction. If he had stayed where he was one of the slugs would surely have found its mark but, as soon as he had called, he rolled to his left. He waited until he could see a target and fired off several shots.

A rifle cracked over to his right where Kelly Quintock was concealed and Jason was pleased that, judging from the shout of pain, one of the slugs had found its target, how badly was difficult to tell. Rifle fire was now coming from the window of the shack and the situation was getting out of control.

'I only want the girl,' Jason shouted again when there was silence as he shifted his position once more. 'Send her out an' we'll be on our way.'

More shots followed and he knew something more drastic had to be done. Out of the corner of his eye he saw the sheriff running, crouching low, towards the side of the shack where he thought he could not be seen. But a rifle spat and Jason winced as he watched the sheriff go down. He let off a series of shots, aiming at the place where the shooter was concealed. As he did so he was relieved to see the sheriff roll behind the shelter of a fallen log.

'Can't be too bad,' he muttered as he considered his next move.

There was no way he could approach the front of the building over the open ground without being shot and he shifted his gaze to his left where the tree line continued until it reached the trail beyond the shack. If he could reach that and cross the trail he could maybe approach the gunnies from the other side.

'Send out the girl an' we'll let you leave peaceful,' he shouted as he set off between the trees. He reloaded as he ran.

The answer from one of the hard-cases came as a roar. 'Throw down yer weapons and show yerselves an' we might let ya live.'

He had expected this and didn't stop to pay it any heed, trying to make as little noise as possible as he angled round. When he reached the edge of the trail he paused; then, crouching, raced across to the shelter of the rocks.

As soon as he reached them he realized his mistake when a hoarse voice, full of triumph, grated, 'That's far enough. Shuck yer gun an' walk slowly t'wards the hut.'

As he did so he felt his Colt being withdrawn from its holster. 'Think yer smart, doncha?' A rifle barrel prodded him in the back to help him on his way. 'We've met before, ain't we? Well, I reckon this is yer lucky day.'

At that moment there was the sharp sound of a gunshot close by and Jason heard the grunt of pain from the man behind him as the bullet struck home. For half a second Jason stood still, then he whirled. His captor lay still in the dirt. Blood from the wound in his chest had begun to seep through his shirt.

Without knowing where the shot had come from or who had fired it he scooped up his rifle and hurled himself into the cover of the rocks. Looking about he saw a figure above him, kneeling on a ledge. It was Lew.

Jason signalled his thanks but could see the danger Lew was in now that he had given away his position. He was in full view of the second outlaw. 'Get down!' he yelled but the warning was too late. Lew was hurled sideways as a slug struck him. Slowly he teetered on the edge of the rock and rolled over the edge. He was dead before he hit the ground.

Anger overcame caution. Jason rushed forward, rifle spitting lead and a roar coming from his throat. He knew where the shooter lay concealed. At the same time he saw the sheriff come round the corner and duck under the window before Zeb or Duke could get off a shot.

The second shooter stood no chance, and he too lay unmoving in the dust.

The sheriff's face was white with pain as he sank to his knees and Jason now saw that the bullet had pierced his side. 'Is it bad?' he asked.

'Flesh wound. No bones broken but I'm losin' blood,' Kelly replied through gritted teeth. 'I'll live, though.'

They both turned their attention to the shack.

'Zeb!' Jason shouted. 'You've got one chance of stayin' alive. You and Duke come out now with yer hands up or we come in an' get you.'

'I'll kill the girl.' Zeb's voice was harsh with bravado or fear. Maybe both.

'Don't be a fool, Zeb,' the sheriff said. 'Come out peaceful an' you won't be hurt.'

Silence followed and they looked at each other. 'This sticks in my craw but we'll have to let them go,' Jason murmured. He turned towards the shack. 'OK, Zeb. Here's our offer. Let Grace come out an' you can ride off. We won't stop you.'

'How do I know I kin trust you?'

'You have our word. Let's see you, but don't make any sudden moves.'

They waited some more with their eyes on the door.

Zeb's voice reached them again. 'OK. But we've got a condition, too.'

'You're not in a position to make conditions.'

'Yeah, well, nothin's gonna happen unless you let us take our guns. It's dangerous fer a man to travel without protection.'

Jason thought hard. It went against common sense to allow the men to be armed but the last thing he wanted was a long stand-off. 'Do I have yer word you'll not use them agin us?'

'Yeah.'

'Both of you?'

'I said so, din't I?'

'Are we really gonna let him go?' Kelly asked.

'No choice, but we'll need to check on Grace first.'

They need not have worried. After a

minute Grace stepped out of the shack closely followed by Zeb and Duke who was limping badly from the slug he'd received earlier. She walked unsteadily towards them while Zeb and Duke made for their horses and the sheriff kept his Winchester levelled at him in case of tricks.

'You all right?' Jason asked as Grace almost fell into his arms.

She nodded and fingered the bruise on her chin where Zeb had hit her. 'Am I glad to see you.'

'It's becoming somethin' of a habit.' Jason said with a smile. He glared at Zeb. 'What in hell did ya think you were doing?'

Zeb glared back. 'This ain't no business o' yours.'

'Don't think this is the end of the matter,' Jason grated. 'I've gotta let you go but we'll be meetin' up again.' As an afterthought he said, 'You can do one thing fer me when you see your friend, Adam. Tell him I'd like to meet him. One to one. Will you do that?'

Zeb seemed to have regained some of his courage. 'Yeah, I'll tell him. An' if he don't kill you, I will.'

Jason sighed. 'I guess you'll try. Just tell him I'd be obliged if he'd return my Henry. You got that?'

Without answering Zeb set his horse at a fast clip up the trail. Duke followed. Reluctantly Jason watched them go.

'You fit to ride?' he asked Grace.

'Take more'n a clip on the jaw to stop me. Are we gonna follow them?'

Jason grimaced. 'Wish we could, but I've got three bodies to take back an' the sheriff's not fit fer much. Think you could look after his wound? If we can stop the bleeding an' get him mounted we should be all right, but there's a long way to go an' we gotta move along.'

He glanced at the sky and let his gaze settle on the bodies. 'Best if we do most of our travellin' by night.'

While Grace saw to the sheriff Jason wrapped the dead in whatever coverings

178

he could find. He heaved the two outlaws across the saddles of their mounts, then took special care when he came to Lew. 'Dammit, you saved my life,' he muttered. 'An' here I am havin' to cart you home like this. Why the hell did ya double back?'

11

At the outlaws' hideout Adam had become angry when he saw that Frankie and Jo-Jo had allowed themselves to take lead in their gun fight with Jason and Grace. Wounded men were not best equipped to take part in raids. He had therefore dispatched them to clear out the shack, believing it to be no longer safe as a meeting place.

Billy felt he was being blamed for something that was not his fault and had tried to stay out of the way. He was coming to realize that he had not been accepted by the gang and never would be. Well, if they wanted it that way he would take action on his own. He made plans to leave at the first chance he got.

It came shortly after the overnight storm, when most of the outlaws were occupied. With Frankie and Jo-Jo away Adam had led the remaining men on a raid, leaving only one at the hideout with orders to keep Billy in sight at all times.

In the event it had been easy to slip away. His departure, although he couldn't know it, had coincided with Zeb and Duke's journey to the shack. He was confident that once on the trail he would not be followed, not least because he had pistol-whipped his guard before he left. To be certain that he was not being followed he checked his back trail often.

He grinned, his face set with determination. To ensure that he stood less chance of meeting anyone who knew him he soon left the main trail and took another route, an old owlhoot trail. He was in no hurry, savouring the moment to come when he would face one of the men who had ruined his family.

He camped for the night, confident that he was well concealed and set off after sunup next morning, planning to arrive at the CB ranch at sundown when there would be fewer men to prevent his approach.

He crested a rise and his excitement rose as the ranch house came into view, a mere hundred yards away. The western sky was orange and red. The air was still. He sat and thought how his pa used to love this time of day when the sweet smells of the prairie scented the air. At last he urged his mount forward, expecting to be challenged as he drew nearer.

To his surprise there was no one to impede his progress, all hands seeming to be busy elsewhere. He rode in at an easy pace. A grim expression matched the coldness in his eyes and mirrored the inner feeling of triumph as he contemplated what he was about to do. Revenge lent a sharp taste to the prospect of avenging the death of his parents.

He approached from the rear, then circled the building until he had a view of the front. When he was still some twenty yards away he saw the figure on the porch where the last rays of sun cast long shadows. If that man was Carter Brown this was going to be easier than he'd thought. He urged his mount right up to the rail and sat there, staring into the eyes of the rancher who had driven his family away. For the space of half a minute neither man said a word. A tight smile stretched across Billy's face.

Carter Brown was seated in a rocking chair. He was finely dressed in a dark-grey suit and white silk shirt tied at the neck with a black cravat. A thin woollen cover lay over his knees. His hands were clasped in his lap, the fingers inter-twining with each other nervously.

'Who the hell're you?' he asked. 'Don't reckon I know you. Have you brought news of my daughter?'

'Don't know nothing about your daughter,' Billy growled. 'But I remember you well, old man. It's bin a long time coming but now's the time to say ya prayers.' He fingered the Colt resting on his hip.

'Don't reckon I know what you're talking about,' Carter Brown said evenly. 'You come ridin' in here, lookin' fer trouble and then what? You have a mind to kill me? Fer why?' A .45 lay on the table by his side but he made no attempt to reach for it.

Billy slid easily to the ground and mounted the four wooden steps. His eyes were deep-set, shaded by the rim of his Stetson. He studied the rancher, noticing that his face was drawn and more lined than when he'd known him years ago.

'Let me remind you,' he said. 'My memory's as clear as the day it happened. I hadn't reached my tenth birthday when you ran us off our land. Ma, Pa and me. Not s'prised ya don't cotton on to who I am. I've growed up since then. But I recall it well enough, the gunshots, the fire, the panic as you burned our homestead down.'

Carter Brown drew heavily on his cheroot and let the smoke curl up lazily into the warm evening air before he spoke. 'You've strayed off the trail, young man, if you b'lieve I had anything to do with what happened to you and ya family. Looks to me like you've had a wasted journey.'

Billy set his jaw. He'd waited a long time for this moment, planned it, dreamed about it. As he looked about him he was aware of the beauty and majesty of the landscape, the rolling grassy plains, the blue mountains rising in the distance.

It was in these surroundings that he should have had his home, the place where his ma and pa could have lived out their lives tending to their small homestead. Carter Brown had taken all this from him.

He looked again into the eyes of the man in front of him and a chill ran down his spine at the thought of what was going to happen. 'Yeah, you figured right. I'm gonna kill you whether you wanna remember me or not. You used to be good with that gun of yourn, so on your feet. I'm callin' ya.'

Carter Brown didn't move. 'Not so fast, young man. I've told you, I don't know who you are and why you've ridden into my ranch with hatred in your heart.'

'Think back, old man. My pa owned the farm over by Horseshoe Pass. Bought an' paid for. Lush grass, plenty of water, everything he needed. 'Cept you reckoned you needed it, too. Your gunnies drove us off. We soon found out the sheriff was in your pay an' would do nothing to help us. His turn'll be comin' quite soon. Remember now? 'Cos I want that to be the last memory you'll ever have.'

The rancher's expression changed slightly. 'You're mistaken. I may be guilty of many bad things but any land I have was paid for. You must understand that building up a success-ful ranch requires hard decisions. I've worked hard an' played fair all my life. If your pa sold his land to me then it's because he wanted to, not because I forced him. You were too young then to understand. Times were difficult for families like yours.'

Billy's mouth twisted into a grin. 'I don't believe you, old man. Men like you have no honour, no sense of fair play. You play by your own rules. Well, now I'm playing by mine.

'Before I put a slug in you I want you to know why you're gonna die. Right here. Right now. My name is Billy Manning. My pa was Eli Manning. That jog yer memory some?'

'You've let the idea of revenge eat into your soul,' the rancher said. 'I've no mind to swap lead with you. I suggest you turn round an' ride away before you do anything you regret. I've already told you what I know. I bought up a whole heap of land back then an' I paid good dollars for all of it.'

Billy's brows drew together in a deep furrow. There was an unreal feeling of calm about the confrontation. 'Tell me one thing,' he said. 'The sheriff, Kelly Quintock. How much did you pay him?'

'Seems like you're determined to remember things that never happened, kid. You've got it all wrong. Kelly Quintock used to be a good, honest sheriff. Probably still is, though he's a mite older now like we all are. He kept the peace an' people respected him for it.'

'I ain't no kid, old man. I was young when you drove us out, but since then I've growed up fast. So what's it to be? Die standin' up or sat in your chair? Make up yer mind.'

Carter Brown shrugged his shoulders but still remained seated. 'I've no more patience listening to your wild stories. I'm waiting for my daughter an' I'd be obliged if you'd leave now.'

Billy gazed into the rancher's eyes and failed to see any remorse there. Well, whether he remembered or not his time had come. Today, now, would be the reckoning. 'Get on yer feet,' he grated.

The rancher still made no move. 'D'you think I care about dying? If you've a hankerin' to shoot me then let's get on with it. But you'll have to help me. You may not've noticed but I'm stuck in this chair o' mine until someone lifts me out of it.'

Billy raised his eyebrows in disbelief. 'I can't shoot ya while you're sittin' down,' he said.

A taut smile stretched the rancher's lips. 'Well, then, hoist me up and lean me agin that post. Then hand me that pistol unless you wanna shoot an unarmed man.'

Billy hesitated, then did as he was asked, surprised at the lightness of the man.

They faced each other at a distance of five yards, too close to miss. Carter Brown held his pistol loosely by his side. Billy's gun was still holstered and he hesitated. 'Damn it to hell,' he growled. 'Use yer gun!'

'Draw when you're ready,' the rancher growled, a look of resignation on his face. 'When my gun points to your heart I intend to pull the trigger whether you've drawn or not. One of us won't be standing when this is over. Back off now or make your play. Choice is yours.'

Billy waited until the last moment. He drew, thumbed the hammer and fired. Both guns went off simultaneously.

12

The first part of the ride back from the shack had not been as difficult as Jason had expected. Before setting off they had stayed long enough to fill their bellies and rest the horses, all the time keeping a watch in case Zeb took a notion to return.

Grace proved to be an efficient nurse as she cleaned and dressed the wound in the sheriff's side. In spite of the rough treatment she had received at the hands of Zeb she was in good spirits, although the swelling of her jaw caused her smile to be somewhat lopsided.

A short while before sundown they began their journey. Jason led with Grace and the sheriff following, trailing behind them the three horses carrying the dead bodies of Lew and the outlaws. Jason eased back where the trail was wide enough and settled in next to Carter Brown's daughter. There was a lot he knew about her pa's activities, and those of Zeb. Much he suspected, but he wanted more.

'Do you wanna tell us what happened?' he asked.

'You know most of it,' Grace said. 'Zeb is my half-uncle, although some say that might not be true. I don't know. He's held a grudge against my pa ever since he realized the ranch was not going to be left to him. It'll come to me when Pa is ready, so Zeb resents me even though I've done him no harm. I think Pa was never sure about him.'

Jason waited for her to go on. When she didn't he said, 'I was bein' set up by both your pa and Zeb, wasn't I? Zeb recognized me as a look-alike for the outlaw, Adam One-ear, after Duke picked a fight with me back at the saloon. That's why he stopped the fight. I was to be killed when the time was right. They'd have to've cut off my ear an' I'm rather attached to that. I b'lieve your pa might've bin in on that crazy scheme,' he added slowly, 'though mebbe reluctantly.'

Her eyes held his and he saw in them a deep sadness. 'Seems like it,' she said at last. 'I knew nothing about their plans an' I can hardly believe it now. I must've closed my eyes to anything I didn't want to believe. I'm ashamed for myself and Pa. If it means anything at all I know he's ashamed, too.'

It was a while before Grace spoke again. 'He's not been well for some time. I think he knows he's dying, though he'll never speak about it. There's something in his past that he's ashamed of but he won't tell me about that either. I'm worried what he might do now this has all come out into the open. I should never have left him alone.'

'Weren't your choice. We'll soon have you back with him. You are what he cares about most of all.' He understood her fear but he had to get to the bottom of the mystery.

There was another reason, too, for

his wanting to understand Grace's part in all this. Every time he looked at her his heart beat faster. He wanted to hold her again, to feel her soft body against his, to protect her. He had no idea of her own feelings towards him. Gratitude, perhaps, for saving her life? It would not be enough.

They rode in silence, having to travel single file where the trail narrowed. When he was able he rode beside her again.

'Substitutin' a dead body fer an outlaw an' tryin' to claim the reward isn't usually a good idea,' he said softly. 'That's 'cause the outlaw is very much alive an' active. Yet that's what Zeb was aimin' to do. Don't make much sense.'

The sheriff who had been sitting his horse with his head dropped forward suddenly sat up straight. 'It makes sense to me,' he said.

'Thought you was out of it,' Jason laughed.

The sheriff forced a grin. 'Yeah, I thought so, too. But I aim to stay in the land o' the living a while longer. Adam One-ear is a dangerous outlaw,' he explained. 'He kills an' robs an' he don't care who gets hurt in the process. But, 'sfar as I see it his success has made him the target for all kinds of bounty hunters and young men who want to prove somethin'. The law is also makin' life difficult for him. He needs people to think he's dead so he kin start afresh in some other place without bein' hounded.'

His face took on a grim expression. 'He doesn't know it yet but I aim to kill him afore he's much older. There's also the fact that there's a bounty on his head an' that ain't a bad thing.' He slumped forward again.

Jason thought that the sheriff wouldn't be killing anyone for some time, but in that he was wrong.

The shadows had lengthened as they entered a stony part of the trail where it narrowed between two rock faces, which forced them to ride single file. The high sides of the cliffs cut out much of the light and threw back the sound of the horses' hoofs.

Without warning a rifle shot reverberated and a bullet plucked at Jason's sleeve. A sharp pain told him the slug had found flesh.

'Hell,' Jason growled. 'Git under cover.' He leaned across and gave the sheriff a hefty shove that sent him toppling to the ground. At the same time he grabbed the Winchester from the saddle boot and slid from his horse. He was gratified to see that Grace was doing the same. 'What critter wants us dead now?'

More shots followed as he made for the shelter of a large boulder. He dragged the sheriff after him, not caring that he was objecting to the rough treatment as a bullet splintered the rock near his head and sent a shard into his cheek. 'Where's the shooter? Anyone see?' He mopped the blood with his neckerchief.

Grace, crouching beside him, shook her head. Their horses, clearly spooked by the noise, were out in the open, as were the three carrying the dead bodies.

Jason looked about him. 'At least two, I reckon,' he said. 'Stay hunkered. I'll see if I kin get above them.' Keeping low he raced towards the cliff face where another, larger boulder gave promise of better shelter and the possible means of making progress up the cliff face. Bullets followed him, too close for comfort. He glanced back at Grace and saw her exchanging fire with her unseen opponents. He might have expected that she was not a girl to stay hidden for long and he was grateful that she was keeping the shooters pinned down.

Anger welled inside him and his mind worked as he climbed, silent and sure-footed as a mountain lion. He reckoned the bushwhackers were unlikely to be bandits or any of the Adam outlaw band. Yet, whoever it was clearly intended to kill. He'd been shot at from ambush before and that time it had been Zeb and Duke.

Could they have doubled back and waited for them, knowing they would have to travel through the defile? Too late he knew he should not have let them take their weapons. But what choice had there been?

From higher up he could pinpoint where the shots were coming from and, even in the half-light, he could see the two men lying on their bellies lower down on the other side of the trail about forty yards away. He also saw where they had tethered their mounts in a cleft in the rocks.

He knelt, Winchester at his shoulder, and aligned the sights. It would be easy to put lead into both men before they knew what had hit them, but he had to give them the opportunity to give up without a fight.

'I know who you are, ya lying varmints,' he muttered. Then he yelled, 'Lay down yer weapons. I've got ya covered.' He sent a warning shot into the rocks above them.

The shooters had other ideas. Both

adjusted their aim and let off several rounds in Jason's direction. The shots were wild. He took careful aim and put lead into the larger man, which sent him tumbling backwards to roll over the edge and lie unmoving on the ground below.

'Put yer hands up,' he yelled again and sent another shot that splintered the rock at the other shooter's feet.

This time the man obeyed.

'Throw ya weapons over an' then make yer way carefully down to the trail,' Jason ordered. 'I wanna be able to see ya all the way.' He called down to Grace. 'Let me know when you've got him in yer sights an' I'll climb down. Be interestin' to see who we've netted.'

A few minutes later Zeb stood in front of them with his hands raised in the air. There was dust on his clothes and fury in his eyes. 'Damn you to hell!' he growled.

'Not today, I reckon,' Jason said. 'Mebbe it's you who'll be going.'

The sheriff, who was still lying where

he had fallen, raised himself to a sitting position. 'Put a slug in him,' he grated. 'He's not worth wasting time on.' He put a hand down to his bandaged wound. 'Dammit, I'm losing blood again.'

Grace put down her rifle and knelt beside him while Jason considered the position they were in with a wounded man and three dead bodies. Four bodies now that he had shot Duke.

He fingered the lever of the rifle. 'Tempted,' he grinned. 'It's either that or we let him go.' He walked slowly towards Zeb until he stood within inches of him. Suddenly his fist swept up and caught Zeb on the point of his jaw, sending the man staggering back until he sat down heavily in the dirt.

He rubbed his knuckles. 'Heck, I shouldn't've done that, but I feel a whole heap better. What's up with you, Zeb, that you can't see when it's time to quit? Before I decide what to do with you you're gonna wrap Duke up in his bed roll and hoist him on to the back of his horse so we kin take him back to town. Get on yer feet.'

At gunpoint Zeb did as he was ordered. Duke was indeed dead. If the slug hadn't killed him the fall certainly had. Jason gathered up all the weapons and, leading the horses with him, marched Zeb back to where Grace and the sheriff were waiting.

'OK,' he said to his prisoner. 'This is what we're gonna do. You're comin' back to town with us and you're goin' to jail. Then you'll face the circuit judge on charges of murder, kidnappin', rustlin' and any other charges we can think of. Of course, if you tell the law where Adam's hideout is you'll mebbe avoid the rope round yer neck.

'I was sort of hoping you'd be able to tell Adam I wanted to meet him but this is the next best thing. Let's git mounted and cover some more ground.'

The sheriff struggled to his feet but it was clear he was feeling the effects of loss of blood. He let out a cry of pain and lurched against Grace who was trying to assist him. For a moment Jason's attention was diverted and, in those brief seconds, Zeb leaped into the saddle and dug spurs into the animal's flank. The beast set off at a fast pace with Zeb crouched low on its back.

Jason drew his Colt and thumbed the hammer. With his finger about to exert pressure he hesitated and watched as Zeb rode out of range. 'Can't shoot him in the back,' he said. 'Could be he's done us a favour.'

* * *

Zeb, expecting to feel a slug in his back, spurred his horse forward, crouched low over the animal's neck. To his relief and surprise no bullet came his way and there was no sound of pursuit. He eased up on the pace and risked a look behind him. A triumphant smile spread across his face as he realized that a rifle lay in the saddle boot and that he had escaped once again.

As the distance away from his captors

increased the thought of doubling back and lying in wait for them played in his mind. To get back at his enemies so quickly would be rewarding. But as he considered the idea more deeply he shook his head and continued at a steady pace.

He wasn't finished yet, although he could no longer return to the ranch. Adam would surely welcome him now as part of the outlaw gang, especially when he learned that two of his men had been killed. Now was the time for him to reap his reward for all the help he had given to the gang.

At the back of his mind was the thought of the bounty still hanging over Adam's head. The opportunity might yet present itself for him to stake his claim one way or another.

Three hours' riding brought him to the outlaws' hideout. He found Adam resting in the small hut that served as the eating and sleeping quarters of the gang.

'What in tarnation happened to you?'

Adam queried, as he took in Zeb's bruised face and dishevelled appearance.

Zeb had been rehearsing his story as he rode. 'We were ambushed by the sheriff an' his buddies down by the shack. We didn't stand a chance. They got Jo-Jo and Frankie first off. I hit the sheriff but I don't know how bad an' then they got Duke. I was gettin' away when one o' them tackled me an' I had to deal with him. There was nothing else I could do with all o' the others dead.'

Adam was silent, fury building up within him, as he took in what Zeb had told him. 'Dead, you say. You certain of that?'

'Sure as hell.'

'I've already got one wounded man. The young snake I took in split Conroy's scalp an' left in a hurry. Now Jo-Jo an' Frankie. What the hell's goin' on? What were you doin' at the shack?'

Zeb gave a twisted grin. 'I was bringin' the girl to you.'

'What girl? We don't welcome women here.'

From Adam's reaction Zeb wondered if it had been a good idea. 'The rancher's daughter, Grace. Thought you might like to hold her for a sizeable ransom. Or for some other purpose,' Zeb added.

Adam understood but his expression didn't change. 'We kin find our own female company when we need to. So, what happened to her?'

'They took her back.'

Adam looked hard at the other man as the situation became clear. 'So, as I understand it, you let a posse follow you out to the shack where you were holding the girl an' then you ran from the fight while the others were gettin' themselves shot. Is that about it?'

Zeb, realizing that it wasn't far from the truth, tried to change the direction of the conversation. 'One o' them, a drifter by the name o' Jason, seemed to know you. He sent a message.'

'Yeah?'

'Something like he wanted to meet you and would you return the Henry rifle you took from him. Does that make sense?'

'No sense at all,' Adam grunted. 'I've taken firearms off a heap o' people, some dead, others I didn't feel like killin' at the time. Must be one o' them.' He waved a dismissive hand at Zeb. 'Now you're here go an' make yourself useful while I think.'

13

At the CB ranch Billy Manning and Carter Brown stood facing each other, Billy displaying hatred in his eyes, the rancher showing no emotion at all.

Slowly Carter Brown sagged against the rail and his gun dropped from his hand. Billy stood, numbed by his own success.

'How'd ya like a little of yer own medicine?' he growled as the rancher slid down to his knees and then fell back to lie unmoving on the wooden floor.

He was alerted to his danger by shouts from the corral. He'd accomplished what he'd set out to do and now he had to get out fast. His task was not yet complete.

He holstered his gun and leapt into the saddle, giving spurs to his mount as he wheeled about and set off at a fast gallop away from the ranch. He didn't much care if he was followed. His horse was fresh and fast and he had a good start.

A feeling of exhilaration filled him as he headed for the town. He would do what he had to do, then return to the outlaw's hideout. Adam would surely accept him as a full member of the gang again when he told him what he had done.

As night approached he entered Inspiration over the tract of soft waste ground at the rear of the main buildings, avoiding the main street as far as he was able. The timing of his arrival had been chosen with care; the stores were closed, the good citizens were in their homes and the men in the saloon well supplied with liquor.

He knew he might have some time to wait and he needed a place to hole up until he was ready. He'd given some thought as to how he could achieve that and had arrived at a simple plan.

He stabled his horse at the livery.

'See that she's well fed an' rested,' he said. 'I'll prob'ly be wantin' her in a hurry tomorrow.' He walked back down through the back alleys towards the saloon and waited at the rear until he considered the time to be right.

As the night progressed the noise from inside the building increased, voices, honky-tonk music from the overworked piano and some half-hearted singing. He walked down the alley, went into the saloon through the batwings and approached the bar, careful not to attract too much attention. He need not have worried; hardly a head turned in his direction.

'Whiskey,' he said to the barman while his gaze swept around the room.

'You'll be that young buck the sheriff chased outa town.' The barman sized him up with a cynical stare.

Billy smiled disarmingly. 'Yeah. No harm done.'

'You ain't gonna have another go at linin' yer pockets, are ya? I got money in that bank.'

'Rest easy,' Billy said. 'I reckon there ain't no quick way o' getting' rich. I've taken a job out at the CB ranch. I'll be workin' fer my living from now on.' He looked along the bar. 'Don't keep yer other customers waiting.'

When he was alone he deliberately made eye contact with one of the doves employed by the saloon to keep the customers happy. She sidled across to him. 'I've seen you before, haven't I?' she said. 'You lookin' fer company?'

'I reckon.' Billy studied her. 'Depends what you've got to offer.'

She smiled. 'More than you kin handle.'

'Sounds interesting'. He took in her straining bosom, the lines in her face and the strands of greying hair. 'You gotta name?'

'Marley. They call me Marl. Among other things,' she added. 'You're Billy, ain't ya?' There was a simulated coyness in her eyes and voice.

'OK, Marl. I gotta little business to attend to, then I'll be lookin' fer a place to stay. You wouldn't be able to help me out there, would ya? I kin pay whatever you ask.' He made a show of rustling the dollar bills in his pocket. He noticed the gleam that came into her eyes as he did so and guessed that she rarely received such a promising offer.

Marl did not have to think about it for long. 'I gotta two-room clapboard on the edge of town,' she said. 'I can finish work here in about three hours.'

He tried to appear embarrassed. 'Marl, I've never done this sorta thing afore an' I'd be more'n grateful if you'd not tell anyone.'

She looked him up and down with an amused smile. 'Reckon you're quite young, ain't yer? You're in fer the experience of yer life.'

Billy gave her his very best smile and she explained how to get to the small wooden building she called home. 'Three hours,' he said. 'I'll look forward to seein' you there.'

He left the saloon and, still keeping to the shadows of the rear lots where there was little light, made for the eating house. He knew the news of Carter Brown's death would not be long in coming but a full belly was essential. Hunger could make a man careless. Tonight he would have to stay alert and tomorrow he would have to leave town quickly. There would be a long ride ahead of him.

Three hours later he was waiting outside the small building that Marl called her own. Midnight had come and gone. He was there for another thirty minutes before he heard her footsteps approaching. He kept himself concealed until he was sure there was no one with her.

'You're late,' he said. 'Thought I'd be able to rely on you.'

'You can,' she said shortly. 'I'm a working girl. You're not my only customer.'

He shrugged. 'Well, you're here now.'

She produced a key, opened the door and ushered him into the front room. 'It's not much,' she explained, 'but it suits me fine.' She struck a match and lit a kerosene lamp hanging from the ceiling. Its yellow light showed up the sparseness of the furniture.

He looked around. Everything was neat and clean. A table and two chairs were set in one corner, a small stove stood against the far wall and various other items showed that this room doubled as a kitchen and dining area.

Yeah, he thought, it's sure not much but it'll suit me fine as well. He took off his coat, unbuckled his gunbelt and hung them both on wooden pegs hammered into the wall.

'Make yourself comfortable,' she said and stood waiting as if expecting something from him.

'Ten dollars OK?' he asked. It wouldn't have mattered if she'd asked for a hundred. Billy intended to get it all back by the end of the night. He dug his hand into his inner pocket and placed the silver into her outstretched hand.

'That's generous,' she smiled. 'You

get the very best treatment fer that.'

'Best lock the door,' he said. 'Don't reckon on gettin' disturbed.'

'Never needed to lock myself in,' Marl said but handed him the key as she lit the stove and prepared some coffee.

'Best fer a girl to keep herself safe.'

'You're that young feller who tried to rob the bank, aren't you?' she asked. 'What was that all about?'

He shrugged. 'Just gettin' my hand in. Anyway, this town owes me, the boss of the CB Ranch an' the sheriff in partic'lar.'

He felt Marl's eyes on him as she tried to figure out exactly what he meant. 'D'you wanna talk about it?' she asked.

He hesitated, not certain how much he could tell her. 'It's a while ago now,' he said. 'They may've forgotten me but sure as hell I ain't forgot them. I gave Carter Brown cause to recall what he'd done an' I'll make damn sure the sheriff does the same before I kill him too.'

He sucked on his lip, sure now that he had said too much as he saw the light of understanding and fear in Marl's eyes.

'What have you done to Carter Brown?'

Billy rubbed his hand through his hair as if trying to recall. 'Let's just say he won't be turnin' nobody else off their land,' he said.

'You killed Carter Brown?' She drew in a sharp breath and stepped away from him. 'Is that why you asked me to give you a bed for the night? You're hiding?' She stepped to the door and made to turn the key. 'I want you outa my house an' you can keep your money.' She slammed the silver down on to the table.

Billy grabbed her arm, digging his fingers into her flesh. 'No need fer that. We can just stay here till sunup, then I'll be gone if'n you give me your word you'll give me time to get away before you go raisin' your voice down the street.'

She tried to pull away. 'You're hurting,' she said angrily. 'I'll promise whatever you want.'

But he knew it was hopeless even if she did mean what she said. Although he had no intention of harming this woman he knew he had to keep her quiet.

His grip on her arm tightened. 'What does this town owe you, anyway, Marl? D'ya think people respect you for what you do? They use you, that's all.'

'At least I didn't do no harm to no one,' she whimpered. 'Why d'you have to kill?'

He realized from her tone that there was only one way to make sure he could sleep easy. He needed rest. Tomorrow he would need all his wits about him. He would have to forgo the night of passion that she had offered him.

He reached for a length of thin rope he had noticed on the wall. 'Sorry, Marl. You an' me'll have to wait for another time. I don't aim to hurt you but I've gotta tie you up so's you don't get any ideas. You'll be comfortable on ya bed s'long as you don't struggle.'

But Marl did struggle and he was surprised how strong she was. Before he had her secure he had suffered several punishing blows to his face and body and his nose ran blood down the front of his shirt. Teeth marks cut deep on his arm.

'Goddamn it, Marl, what d'ya think yer doing?' He stifled her scream by stuffing cloth into her mouth and then tying a strip over her lower face. Her eyes glared at him with fear and anger.

'There, that'll do,' he told her when she was finally trussed up and silent. 'It's only fer the night. I'll be gone first thing an' I'll leave word fer someone to come and untie you. Sorry I have to do this but it's fer the best.' He dragged a cover over her and, with a last glance to make sure she was breathing, left her in spite of her pleading look.

In the front room he helped himself to a mug of coffee. Then he lay down on the floor and, with his coat rolled up under his head, he shut his eyes. Marl moaned for a while but even that noise stopped and he drifted into a fitful sleep.

He awoke as light seeped in through the small window. The hard wooden floor had stiffened his joints and he eased himself to his feet, listening to any noise that might indicate that his presence had been discovered. Even Marl was quiet. Too quiet. Her flesh was cold to the touch. He bent low over her face but could detect no breath. He stood for several minutes over her dead body, emotions fighting with each other.

'Dammit, Marl,' he muttered. 'Weren't my intention to kill you.' But the deed had been done and he couldn't waste time regretting something that couldn't be undone. He had more important things to concern himself with and he set about getting ready for the task ahead. He covered her face with the sheet and left her where she lay.

14

It was a sombre group, headed by Jason, that continued the journey to Inspiration with one wounded man and four dead strung out in a line. They continually watched their back trail although Jason considered the idea of Zeb following them was now unlikely. The young moon, casting deep shadows from the rocks and outcrops, gave cause for caution.

Some distance from town, as the stars faded at the approach of dawn, the trail split, one way leading to the CB ranch, the other into Inspiration. Jason reined the party in.

'I reckon you should go tell your pa what's bin happening,' he told Grace. 'I'll manage from here on in. The doc'll be my first call, then the undertaker. Then possibly a cold beer, a bath an' a hot meal. And mebbe catch up on some sleep. We'll meet up with each other later. An' you'd best get something on that bruise. It's lookin' real cute. Quite attractive in fact.'

Their eyes met and held. 'I can't thank you enough for all you've done,' she said simply. 'I owe you.' She brought her horse alongside his, stretched out her hand and rested it briefly on Jason's shoulder.

'You don't owe me nothing,' Jason insisted. 'I'm just glad you're all right.'

She leaned across and kissed him, then turned her horse and set it down the trail without looking back. There was a wistful look on Jason's face as he watched her until she was out of sight. She was certainly easy on the eye, graceful, elegant, wild with her long hair flowing out behind her. Yet she had proved herself to be tough and capable with horse and gun. And probably with men.

Wearily he urged his convoy on.

It was inevitable that his entrance to the town would draw attention, leading as he did five horses, four of them with bodies draped over their backs. He was right. The worthy townsfolk who were out and about early enough stared at the progress of the solemn procession, headed by Jason and the sheriff, who by this time had recovered enough to sit up straight.

'Someone get the undertaker,' Jason shouted. Several people hurried to do his bidding.

He made straight for Doc MacReady's where, as he was directed, he slid the sheriff off his horse, helped him into the house and through into the room set up as a surgery. He heard a muttered, 'I kin walk by myself,' in his ear.

The doc, surreptitiously wiping the remnants of his breakfast from his lips, raised his eyebrows but asked no questions as he set to work on his patient, while Jason waited in another room. A smell of iodine and carbolic lingered in the air.

'Bad, but not serious,' the doc announced after about fifteen minutes.

'No great damage. He's lost blood but it looks worse than it is. No bones broken. If I know Kelly he'll be wanting to be up and about before he's ready.'

'That's how I read the man,' Jason agreed. 'I'll come back an' see him later if you can keep him rested fer a while.'

'As soon as he hears what's been going on I won't be able to hold him,' the doc said.

'He knows everythin' I know,' Jason said, a little confused that the doc should think otherwise.

'News travels fast,' the doc observed. 'Nobody seems to know who the killer was. Fletcher's gone out to the ranch to see what he can dig up.'

Now Jason furrowed his brow in concern. 'What killin' are we talking about?'

'Why, Carter Brown of course. I'd no idea you ain't heard. Happened last night apparently while most of the hands were out searching for Carter's daughter. They say that some varmint rode in as open as you like and shot him down on his own porch. He rode off afore any of the hands could give chase.'

Jason's mind was working. Who would want to kill the rancher, and why? His first instinct was to high-tail out to the ranch to offer some support to Grace. But he realized she was a capable young lady and had some good men around her. She might even resent his interference, especially if she thought he considered her to be helpless.

'Any ideas who did it?' he asked. Although he could have made a suggestion as to who the shooter might be he held his tongue.

'People are talking,' the doc said. 'You know how it is. They'll make up stories when they don't know the facts. They say Carter Brown made a lotta enemies in his younger days when he was building up the ranch. Mebbe his crimes have come home to roost. Now tell me how Kelly got shot. Seems to come natural to him.'

Jason told him how they'd found

Grace, how Luke had been shot and Zeb had escaped. 'He won't be returning,' Jason told him.

'Just as well without him,' the doc commented, 'though he seems to've been a good ramrod by all accounts. With Duke and Lew gone too, Grace'll have her hands full. She's a competent young lady though I doubt she's up to running the ranch on her own.'

'Yeah,' Jason said thoughtfully. 'Reckon she'll need help.'

He thanked the doc, allowed the doc's wife to put a dressing on his arm, and set off to unload the bodies waiting patiently outside. He hadn't far to go. Seth Edwards, the undertaker, had not had much work lately and here were four customers all at once. He was quickly at the scene and met Jason as he stepped out on to the boardwalk.

'They've bin on the trail for a while,' Jason warned him. 'Three o' them I don't care much about but one of 'em is Lew from the CB an' I owe him. I'd like him treated special.'

His first stop was at the livery to have his sorrel cared for. It had covered many miles and needed food and a rest as much as he did. His next call was to the saloon where he reckoned a shot of Turley's Mill might set him up for a good meal and some shut-eye.

There were few customers at that time of the morning and no calico girls in attendance. Only the barman, busy polishing the counter, was looking for company. Jason was in no mood for talking and he tipped back the whiskey in one quick swallow, feeling it burning down his throat and into his empty belly.

He went from there to the eating house further up the street and ordered a large meal of porridge and honey, followed by ham and eggs and hunks of brown bread.

There were already four or five other early customers at the tables and it took Jason only a minute or so to recognize the stained overalls and thick eyebrows of Hal Skandy, the proprietor of the

Inspiration Clarion.

The man waved to him, beckoning him over. 'Don't rightly like eatin' on my own,' he said as Jason pulled back a chair and sat down. 'Hear you didn't take my advice.'

'What advice might that've bin?'

'As I remember I suggested you kept yerself clear of the CB Ranch an' Zeb in particular.'

Jason rubbed his chin as he thought on it. 'Mighty good advice,' he grinned. 'Seems like I shoulda taken heed.'

'An' the lovely Grace?' Hal queried. 'As I heard it you've bin seein' quite a lot of her.' His grey eyes held a twinkle.

Jason spooned a mouthful of porridge and swallowed thoughtfully. 'She's a great gal, sure enough. Could be interested in her but I don't reckon she's a mind to go fer a drifter like me.'

'You could be right. I've told you afore what she's like with men and she's had plenty of practice avoiding the clumsy advances of the young bucks hereabouts.'

'I'm not a young buck,' Jason said. 'An' what with everything that's bin going on I'm gettin' older by the minute.'

'Yep, there's a lot bin happening since you hit town.' Hal had finished his meal and leaned back with a mug of coffee in his ink-stained hand. 'Want to tell me the whole story? Make a good front page.'

Jason pondered. 'Yeah, I can let you have some of it,' Jason said. 'It'll make interesting reading. But it ain't over yet. Someone's gotta pay fer shootin' Carter Brown.'

'Someone sent fer the marshal from Yellow Creek but by the time he gets here the trail's likely to've gone cold.'

Jason came to a decision. 'Then it's up to us to find the shooter an' mebbe bring Zeb in to face the judge.' As he tucked into the ham and eggs he began to tell his story, to which Hal listened without interruption. 'You've not taken any notes,' he said when he had finished.

'Don't need to,' Hal told him. 'Gotta memory soaks up facts like rain on a dry prairie. The next edition should be good.' As he got up to leave he added, 'By the way, I saw that young feller last night, the one who tried to rob the bank. Looked like he didn't wanna be seen, sneakin' down the side alleys.'

'Hell,' Jason said. 'I'd forgot about him. Wonder what he's up to.' He paid his bill and they left together, Hal to his trusty printing press, Jason making for the sheriff's office where he hoped he might find the deputy, Fletcher, if he'd finished his enquiries at the ranch. There was an urgency to his step. After that he'd aim for Rosie's place, where he still had a room and he could maybe take a rest.

★   ★   ★

Billy took his time before leaving the safety of Marl's house and was therefore not aware of Jason's entry into the town with his cargo of dead bodies

228

and the flurry of activity that followed. He checked his Colt, lit the stove and made himself some coffee before he let himself out of the door, carefully closing and locking it behind him and taking care not to be seen.

It was now late morning and the main street was busy, but at this moment he wasn't a fugitive although he knew he was soon to become one. He collected his horse from the livery and walked it openly to the front of the sheriff's office where he tethered it to the hitch rail.

The door was ajar. He had expected to have to wait until the sheriff returned from his investigation at the ranch but he drew a deep breath, climbed the three steps on to the boardwalk, pushed the door open and took a step inside.

The sheriff, appearing pale and clearly in discomfort, was leaning back in his old swivel-chair, sucking on a cigar and nursing a glass of whiskey.

The lawman looked up, annoyed at the interruption, as Billy came further into the room. 'Well, well,' he said. 'Didn't think I'd be seein' you agin. Is it you I have to thank fer the groove in my scalp?' He didn't miss the fact that his visitor pushed the bolt across the door.

'If I'd fired the shot that groove would've bin several inches deeper,' Billy told him with a vicious grin. His face was clear of expression except for the wild look in his eyes. 'Nope, I guess you were a mite lucky then but yer luck's just about to run out.'

He dragged the wooden chair over and sat so that he was facing the sheriff from across the desk. He swept his Colt from its holster and pointed it unwaveringly at the lawman's chest. 'You sure look as if someone tried to put a slug in you. Well, there's some more lead on the way.'

The sheriff stared into those cold eyes and realized how close he was to death. He'd faced many dangerous situations where his life had been on the line and he had survived. He'd seen it all, outdrawn or outsmarted many who'd thought to bring his life to a sudden end. So far. He leaned back in his old leather chair, placed his feet on the desk, laid his hands on his lap and let the pungent smoke of his cheroot drift into the air.

'Yeah, seems as if people like taking pot-shots at me and you've come here to do the same,' he observed drily. The hard steel of his eyes fixed on the younger man, holding his attention. He was conscious of the Colt pointing at him and didn't cotton to the idea of having his retirement brought forward in this way. 'What d'ya want from me?'

'You killed my pa an' my ma. Carter Brown drove him off our land an' you did nothing to help. Fact is you let it happen. Yep, you killed my family, though you didn't actually pull the trigger. Now I'm gonna kill you.'

The sheriff clearly reckoned that while he kept Billy in conversation there was a chance he could end the confrontation peacefully. 'You've got it

231

all wrong, son. Nobody killed your pa. You're talkin' about some years back. Things were different then. I recall your family were struggling to make a living and your pa was glad to sell out. That's all there was to it.

'You're on the wrong trail. I upheld the law, that's all. An' the law was on the side of the rancher. Mebbe you were too young then to understand.'

The gun wavered as Billy's finger tightened. 'I was old enough to know exactly what happened. And I'm not your son. Say yer prayers 'cos talkin's finished.'

But the sheriff hadn't finished. While there was talking there was still hope that this would end without bloodshed, his or Billy's. 'OK.' He shifted slightly in his chair. 'If you're minded to pull the trigger let me give you some advice first. If you want to continue down the path of a gunslinger there's only one possible end. You'll either have a rope round yer neck or a slug in yer guts. Either way you'll end up dead.'

'Yeah, I'm sure you believe what you're tellin' me but I'm not hankerin' to die young.'

'Neither am I, son. I'm not yet ready to meet my Maker. I see you've grown harder in just a few days. What's it to be? Hand over that pistol of yourn or face a short life.'

Billy snarled. 'Yeah, I've had to learn real fast. I've settled the score with Carter Brown an' now it's your turn to pay fer what you did.'

'You shot the rancher?'

'Yep. Gave him a chance, though. More'n he gave my pa.'

'Not much of a chance, was it? He's a cripple.'

Billy nodded. 'Yeah. He's a dead one now.'

'If you shot Carter Brown the best thing you can do is give yersel' up. I'll speak for you at the trial.' He leaned forward and the chair creaked.

Billy's gun shook alarmingly. 'No sudden moves! If you've nothin' more to say I'll finish the job I came to do and hightail it outa here.'

The sheriff drew heavily on his cigar, flooding the office with blue smoke. 'The hell you say! Killin' a law officer is a serious crime in these parts. Mebbe you'll be able to argue self-defence but if you pull that trigger it'll be murder. You'd be caught fer sure and strung up.'

Billy gave a tight grin. 'An' if I don't shoot you I'll be caught anyways.'

'You'd have a fair trial. I'd see to that.'

'Not in this town, I wouldn't. I'd rather take my chances out there.' He gestured with his thumb.

The sheriff swallowed hard as he recognized the light in Billy's eyes. 'Mind if I take a slug o' liquor. I'm kinda parched.' He reached for the bottle, poured himself two fingers of the amber liquid into his glass.

A speck of spittle appeared at the corner of Billy's mouth. 'You're fond of ya liquor. That drink's gonna be yer last.'

'Mebbe,' the sheriff drawled. 'But I always take a drink before I shoot some critter who's bin threatening me.' He downed the whiskey in one swallow.

A shiver of doubt appeared in the young man's eyes. 'You ain't about to shoot no one.'

'Nope?' the sheriff said and pulled the trigger of the gun fixed under the desk. The force of the bullet slammed Billy backwards until he hit the wall behind him. A hole appeared where his groin had been and blood spattered the floor and boarding.

The sheriff drew a deep breath and refilled his glass. 'Yep, an' I often have a drink *after* I kill someone.' He tipped the contents down his throat with evident satisfaction before he levered himself to his feet and left the office on his way to the undertaker.

Before he had taken more than a few paces he saw Jason striding towards him.

'Heard the shot,' Jason said as he came up. 'Sounded like a shotgun.

What was that all about?'

Kelly Quintock smiled wearily. 'It was. Billy Manning was on the wrong end when it went off. He had a lot to learn but he's past any hope of doing that now.'

He went on to explain how he'd had no choice but to pull the trigger. 'Didn't want to. That young man could've led us to Adam One-ear and got off with a light sentence if he'd had a mind to.'

'What're you doing up and about?' Jason queried. 'Doc was s'posed to keep you quiet.'

'I'm the law around here, as I keep tellin' everyone,' Kelly grated. 'The doc ain't orderin' me what to do!'

The two men walked slowly together towards Seth Edward's workshop. Jason shrugged. 'What was he playing at?'

'You heard about Carter Brown?'

'Yeah. That's a shock. Don't know who did it yet, do we?'

Kelly gestured back towards his office. 'That young varmint was eaten up with vengeance. He figured to get back at Carter Brown an' me by shootin' us both. It didn't work out that way an' now we're left with another body for Seth to take to Boot Hill.'

'There's bin too much killing,' Jason said. 'But it sticks in my craw that the coyotes who caused it all are still out there.'

Kelly Quintock sent a stream of tobacco juice into the dust. 'Give me time an' I'll be doin' something about that.'

'A posse?'

'We've discussed that before,' the sheriff said. 'A posse won't do it. Adam and his crew'll just melt into the hills if he gets a smell of a bunch of well-armed riders after his scalp. We've gotta be more subtle.'

'We?'

'Thought you might like to tag along. Just you an' me.'

'Sure you're up to it?'

'You sound like the doc.'

Jason, secretly thinking that the idea

was a good one, wanted to show caution. 'Sure, mebbe we could do it. But two of us can't expect to capture the whole outlaw gang.'

'Who said anythin' about capture? Dead or alive the dodger says. I know what I prefer.'

'Are yer gonna deputize me?'

The sheriff grinned sardonically. 'I won't be sheriff when I loose my rifle at 'em.' He touched the silver star on his vest. 'We'll both be plain, ordinary citizens doin' a service for the town.'

'And claimin' the reward?'

'Yep.'

'Bounty hunters, then.'

'Nothin' wrong with bounty hunters,' Kelly said.

'That weren't your view earlier on,' Jason said, grinning.

'A man kin change his mind, can't he?'

They had reached the undertaker's and the sheriff explained how there was another body to take care of in his office. Seth rubbed his hands, a craftsman's hands, and his chubby face split into a grin. 'Business looking up,' he said. 'Hope the town kin afford it.'

'It's messy in there,' Kelly explained. 'I'll get it cleaned up once you've taken the body away. Then mebbe I kin get some of the reports written up or the town council will get their danders up.'

The two men split up, each going his own way, Jason in search of a bed.

15

The next two days were going to be busy. The dead had to be buried, the sheriff's office cleaned up, reports completed and the CB ranch, now without its owner, the foreman and two of its staff, needed to be reorganized.

Jason rode out to visit Grace, expecting to see a young lady out of her depth, distraught at the death of her father and struggling to cope. What he found was a young woman very firmly holding the reins, although without the laughter sparkling in her eyes and with taut lines around her mouth. Her smile when she saw him was genuine enough to make his heart leap.

'I'm so sorry,' he said as she embraced him and held on a little longer than necessary. 'Nobody saw that coming.'

'I blame myself,' she admitted when

they were sitting in the large study so recently occupied by her pa. 'If I hadn't been missing there'd've been more men around to protect him.'

'You were abducted, kidnapped, taken away against your will,' Jason said in some surprise. 'If anyone's to blame it's Zeb and, as things stand at present, he's got away with it.'

Grace laid a hand on his arm. 'Leave it be. Don't feel you're under any obligation to hunt him down on my account or on account of Pa. Wherever Zeb is let him stay there. As long as I don't ever see him again that'll be too soon. Promise me you'll not go after him. Yes?'

Jason evaded answering the question. 'How're the men coping?'

'They've rallied round wonderfully. We're obviously short-handed and we'll have to take on more wranglers, but we're coping at the moment. There's a busy time coming up.'

Jason fancied Grace was looking expectantly at him. 'I'll give whatever help I can,' he said. 'But first there's something I have to do.'

He stayed for the rest of the day, helping out in the corral where Lew would normally have been found, and heading back to Inspiration as the moon made its appearance. At Rosie's he bathed and slept well, the decision to go after the outlaws well set in his mind. His main purpose of going along with the sheriff was to meet Adam One-ear. If, indeed, Adam had saved his life back in the war, Jason would be obliged to prevent Kelly from killing him.

He ate an early breakfast of eggs and bacon and lingered over the final coffee while he worked out his best course of action. He had to find Adam One-ear but he knew it would be both a difficult and dangerous task for one man alone. And, if he succeeded, then what? He also wondered how Grace might fit into his plans for the future.

He thanked Rosie and sauntered out into the morning sun, making for the sheriff's office, still unsure how he was going to proceed. He decided to talk it over with the lawman before reaching any decision.

As he walked he was aware of a shadowy figure standing in one of the alleys. Thinking about it later he realized that his instincts for danger should have kicked in, but his thoughts were elsewhere. With a good-looking young lady to be precise.

What was she going to do now with her father dead and the ranch short-handed? What possible concern was it of his? He had no responsibilities in that direction, had he? In fact he had no responsibilities in any direction.

He could move on now, this very minute, and pursue his own fortune elsewhere, forget about Zeb, Adam One-ear, Kelly Quintock and the good citizens of this town. He had arrived in Inspiration not looking for trouble, yet trouble had found him. He could walk away now with his health and honour intact.

But he knew he couldn't. There were loose ends to tie up. And something, someone else, to keep him here.

At this point his thoughts were interrupted by the hard feel of a gun barrel in the small of his back. 'Down the alley,' a voice grated.

Jason's hand instinctively dropped to his hip.

'And don't even think of goin' fer ya gun.'

He obeyed, hoping that a better opportunity would present itself. 'Who the hell are you?'

'That don't matter,' the voice said, so close to his face that he could smell the sour breath.

In the shade of the alleyway he was ordered to stop. 'Keep yer face to the wall.'

A heavy hand pushing against his shoulders pressed his face against the roughness of the wooden planking.

'What now?' he asked.

'I got a message for ya. From Adam One-ear.'

Jason's heart raced. 'Couldn't you've just told me face to face? What's the idea of trying to put a scare in me?'

'Why d'ya think? I don't like bein' a delivery boy. And because you put slugs in two of my friends. I don't like ya, an' if I had my way I'd put lead into you right now.'

'Well, get on with what you came to tell me an' go back to yer rat-hole.'

The man grunted. 'Three days time. Noon at the shack. Adam'll be there. Come alone.'

Jason sensed the blow coming but he could do little about it. A sudden blinding pain exploded in the side of his head as the pistol slammed into him and he knew nothing more until he regained consciousness to find himself lying face down in the dirt. Without knowing how long he'd been there he pulled himself to his feet and, as his head cleared, felt a thrill of anticipation.

He took a deep breath to clear his head. 'Dang it,' he muttered. 'A note under the door would've bin a mite less painful.'

Against all expectation Zeb had conveyed his message to Adam One-ear. Either that or Zeb was setting a trap for him, knowing that he would not refuse to keep the appointment. The problem was that he was to go alone. He would either have to persuade Kelly Quintock to hold back or go without informing him.

He decided to leave the sheriff for a while and set off for the CB ranch. He felt he owed it to Grace to let her know of this development in case the trap was sprung and he wouldn't be returning. He didn't question in his own mind whether Grace would want to know. He had realized a while back that his own feelings for her had developed to the point where he was keen to continue the relationship. Make it permanent maybe.

'Let me send one of my men with you,' she said when he told her what he intended to do. 'It's sure to be a trap.

How d'you know who sent that message? It could've been Zeb.'

He rubbed his chin. 'I thought of that an' I'll go prepared. I'd be better alone. I know the area now and I'll approach the shack from a different angle. If it is one of Zeb's tricks I think he'll want to spring the trap on his own. If it isn't, then I'll hope to meet the man who saved my life. I can't miss this opportunity. I'll be gone three or four days. Keep the coffee warm for me. An' a bed in the bunk house,' he added.

Grace shrugged. 'I'm sure you know what you're doing but . . . ' she paused, 'be careful.'

Jason thought he might be reading more into those last two words than was intended but he let the idea take root. 'I'll be back,' he said and he meant it. 'I'll need to let Kelly know what I'm gonna do because I promised him we'd go together. He won't be pleased but, considering his state of health, he might not raise too many objections.'

He briefly held Grace's hand before

he turned and remounted, setting off back the way he had come.

No, Jason thought, the sheriff would surely see the wisdom of giving himself time to recuperate from his wounds before tackling another long ride. Jason did not relish the thought of playing nursemaid to a sick man. He would set off at sunup, which would give him plenty of time to take the journey easy and to reach the shack before time.

He was wrong about Kelly Quintock.

'You ain't goin' nowhere without me,' the sheriff said with an edge to his voice. 'I've got more at stake than payin' a debt.'

They were in the sheriff's office, seated opposite each other on either side of the desk. Jason bent down and peered underneath. 'That gun still pointed this way?' he asked.

'Haven't reloaded yet,' Kelly told him with a grin.

Jason studied the man. 'Mebbe that blow on yer head a while ago did more damage than we thought. Jest look at yerself. Like you've bin savaged by a pack o' coyotes. You won't be strong enough to make the journey.'

The lawman sat up straight though Jason could see it was something of an effort.

'Have I gotta remind you agin? I'm the sheriff in this town,' he said, pointing to the star on his chest. 'You'll either do as I say or I'll put you in one of these cells an' keep you there till you see sense.'

'You cain't do that! I ain't broken no law.'

'Believe me, I can do it and I will.'

'On what charge?'

The sheriff thought for a moment, then a smile split his face. 'I'll think on somethin'. Disturbin' the peace'll do till I kin think of somethin' better.'

'I ain't disturbed the peace!'

'Yes you have. You've disturbed mine. Now, are we gonna agree on this? I'm goin' with you.'

Jason agreed, too quickly as he soon realized. 'I've sampled yer hospitality afore and I've no wish to try it agin. So, yep, we go together.'

'In that case,' the sheriff said, grinning more broadly, 'hand over yer hardware.'

'What the hell for?'

'Fer safekeeping till sunup tomorrow. And leave yer horse outside. I'll have it taken to the livery and it won't be released till we're ready to go.'

Jason shrugged. 'You're a hard man, Kelly. But if there's anyone I'd like by my side it'd be you. Remember, I was told to go alone. We'll need to talk about how we're gonna arrange things.'

'Thought you'd see sense.'

16

For the third time in a week Jason and the sheriff had set out along the main trail. That early in the morning dawn had not yet promised the warmth the day would bring. They had huddled in their slickers against the chill and did not speak much to each other until the sun appeared, bringing with it welcome heat.

They eased their mounts to a steady lope. The warmth seemed to loosen their tongues and they began to talk, not of the task ahead but of their plans for the future and their experiences in the past. Jason recounted how, when he had finally recovered from the injury he had suffered in the war, he returned home to find his ma and his younger brother dead and his pa drinking himself to an early grave.

'I gathered up what possessions I

could carry and I hightailed it outa there,' he said. 'I drifted, workin' sometimes, fightin' and killin' when I had to, drinkin' and in general not caring a rattlesnake's kiss for anythin' or anybody.

'By the time I reached Inspiration I'd had enough of aimless wandering and was prepared to settle down. That's why I was int'rested in Carter Brown's offer. I thought, mebbe this is it, this is where I kin put down roots. Well, I've hardly had the opportunity to do that.'

'This place has had its problems,' Kelly agreed. 'I was in the war, too, though I didn't see much fightin'. I came to Inspiration an' took on the job of sheriff. I was young an' keen an' needed the money. I've got old and all that's gone. All I want now is a slice of the reward an' that's what I'm gonna get. Fact is, a slice ain't gonna be enough.'

Jason opened his mouth to reply but thought better of it. The reward was not on his mind and he wondered how he would react if his companion drew a gun on the man who had saved his life.

They camped in the same place as they had on their last journey. The sheriff, who had been showing signs of distress, was slow to move but he uttered no words of complaint.

'We'll easily be there well before noon,' Jason said. But he was concerned about his companion, who was showing clear signs of weakness. 'Can you make it?'

'No need to worry on my account,' Kelly answered, his mouth set in a determined line.

'Right. When we get close you'll need to hold back while I go ahead. If everything's fine I'll signal you.'

'You'll do no such thing,' Kelly grated over his shoulder as he put the saddle on his grey. 'I'm gonna be with you all the way.'

'That's your decision. Don't blame me if you take lead. I was told to come alone.'

They rinsed their utensils in the clear

water of the creek, secured their bedrolls and set off again at sunup. The journey continued in silence until they were within sight of the cabin. There they reined in on the bluff in the shadow of some trees and surveyed the building and the area around it through their glasses. A palomino mare was quietly feeding on the lush grass.

'Smoke coming from the chimney,' Kelly observed. 'Might mean he's waiting for ya inside.'

'Might mean nothin' o' the sort.'

'Might mean Zeb's lyin' in wait to cut us down,' Kelly suggested.

'Or mebbe Adam's a man of his word.'

The sat their mounts, motionless for ten minutes, searching for signs of movement. 'Nothin',' Jason said. 'I'm goin' in.' He checked his guns and the sheriff did the same.

'I'm goin' with ya,' Kelly said.

Jason set his sorrel forward. 'Please yerself.'

They kept their hands in clear sight,

an indication to whoever might be watching that their intentions were peaceful.

Jason's spine tingled as he descended the slope and slowly approached the small shack, anticipating a shot and lead to come winging his way. He sensed the sheriff following behind. The open ground made them easy targets but they continued their steady progress while keeping their hands well away from their weapons.

'Best to go in openly,' he said. 'Whoever's waitin' for us knows this area better'n we do.'

They were within seventy-five yards, their eyes scanning the ground around them, when the shot that Jason had been fearing shattered the peace and the sheriff's Stetson was whisked from his head. 'Dang it!' Kelly muttered.

A voice with the coldness of a north wind rang out into the still air. 'That there's a warning! Any closer an' I'll sure as hell lay ya both in the dirt.'

The shot hadn't come from the cabin

but from the strip of trees edging the creek. Jason realized that anyone who could shoot with that accuracy was someone to be treated with respect. It was possible, of course, that the shooter had aimed to kill and a chill ran down his spine.

They both slid to the ground, sheltering behind their horses.

Jason cupped his hands around his mouth. 'We've come to parlay, not kill,' he shouted hopefully. 'We're comin' in.' To Kelly he said, 'That's not Zeb.'

'You'll do as I tell ya,' the voice said. 'Shuck yer weapons and approach me on foot.'

'Our mounts need water and shade.'

After a brief pause the voice said, 'Lay yer guns on the ground and bring yer horses forward. I'll be coverin' ya all the way so no tricks unless you wanna feed the vultures.'

'Best to follow orders,' Jason said. 'Looks like if he wanted to kill us he could've done.'

They did as they were told, finding

easy access to the water. There they allowed their horses to drink, then ground-hitched them among some lush grass.

The man, still concealed, said, 'Now make yer way out into the open, ten paces then stop.'

As they stood waiting a man appeared suddenly from the deep shadows of trees. He carried a Winchester in the crook of his arm.

When he was closer Jason studied him. This must be the fabled outlaw, he surmised, the man who had spread terror in many states and evaded capture for years. The same man, perhaps, who had carried him from the field of battle those long years ago.

He was tall, lean and muscular, perhaps a few years older than Jason but of similar build, dressed in jeans, black shirt, leather vest and high boots.

The sheriff stared at the two men. 'I see how Zeb got the idea for his crazy scheme,' he said. 'You could be kin.'

Jason nodded. Then, addressing the

outlaw, he said, 'I guess you're Adam.'

'Yep. An' you'll be Jason.' He swept his long hair back from the side of his face, revealing his missing ear.

'I've bin hankerin' to meet you,' Jason said.

'So I understand.' Adam glanced critically at the sheriff. 'An' you are the famous sheriff of Inspiration,' he said with heavy sarcasm.

'You've bin a thorn under my saddle fer long enough,' Kelly growled.

Adam turned the rifle towards him. 'That state of affairs could end right now,' he said. 'I didn't ask you to be here, but since you are — '

'Hold it!' Jason urged. 'He's just a friend. He cain't do nothing to do you harm. Send him on his way. If you kill an officer of the law you'll be hunted down.'

Adam smiled for the first time. 'This far out his silver star don't mean a damned thing. And who'll know that I killed him. No witnesses, you see.' His cold eyes switched to Jason.

'I ain't goin' nowhere,' Kelly said.

'That's jest what I was tryin' to tell ya. 'Cept you might be visiting yer Maker very shortly. I'll think on it.'

They were still standing in the open and the noon sun beat down relentlessly. Perspiration dripped from the sheriff's brow, whether from the heat or fear Jason didn't know. He loosened his bandanna and wiped his brow.

Adam said, 'Yeah, it's a mite hot out here. Guess we'd be better off inside. You first.' He gestured with his rifle.

When they were seated within the relative coolness of the wooden building Jason said, 'You got my message, then?'

'Yep. Din't understand it fer a while. If you're who you say you are I thought you were gone that day fer sure.'

Jason pulled back his shirt to expose the scar from his wound. 'Yet you saved me. Why?'

Adam had visibly relaxed. 'To tell the truth I had in mind to slice yer throat, stick yer with my bayonet. But when I got a good look at you I sort of saw myself lying there. We were very alike so I saved yer hide instead. I took yer Henry, though. Seemed to me you were gonna have no further use fer it. Got rid of it soon after.'

While they talked and drank the coffee that had been brewing on the small stove Jason had been watching the sheriff, who had been particularly quiet. A furtiveness in the man's eyes worried him, causing him to believe he had some trick he was yet to play. Adam seemed to be unaware of it.

Jason rose and held out his hand. 'I've wanted fer long enough to thank you fer what you did. I sure thought my end had come.'

While not relinquishing his grip on the rifle Adam shook his proffered hand with enthusiasm. 'A lotta men on both sides felt the same and weren't so lucky,' Adam said. 'Fer those that survived there weren't many opportunities fer a decent life. My family were killed by guerilla bands. I wasn't obliged to nobody. I did what many others did an' made my fortune outside the law.'

'What now?' Jason asked.

Adam looked at him for a long moment. 'Zeb had some fool scheme to kill you an' make out it was me lying in the dirt. Seein' you now it wasn't such a bad idea. If I was dead no one'd be lookin' to put lead in me an' claim the reward.'

'It would never have worked,' Kelly told him.

'I'm thinkin' about it.' This was said with a belly laugh but there was a thoughtful look on the outlaw's face. 'It would sure take some of the heat off'n me.'

'Dead or alive you're worth a heap o' money,' Kelly suggested.

'Don't git any ideas on that score,' Adam grated, bringing the muzzle of the Winchester up to point at the lawman's chest. 'A load of *hombres* have harboured that thought and, sadly, they didn't live to learn the error of their ways.'

The group fell silent, then all rose and made their way outside again.

Jason said, 'I've done what I came to do. We each go separate ways now. But we're worlds apart, you an' me. If we ever meet again there may be a different ending.'

Out of earshot of the sheriff he added, 'If you want some good advice there's a US marshal on the way here. You won't be dealing with a hick sheriff then. Be best if you got outa this territory an' tried yer luck elsewhere.'

Adam nodded. 'You're mebbe right. I'm glad to've met you both but I hope we'll not run across each other agin. Now, give me time to get on my way.' He walked around the side of the shack, making for his palomino which was standing patiently, already saddled.

Immediately he had turned his back Kelly produced a derringer that had been strapped to the side of his lower leg. 'Hold it right there! Unless you want a hole in yer head,' he yelled. 'This may be a small gun but it'll do a powerful lotta damage.'

As Adam halted in mid stride Kelly said, 'Now drop yer rifle an' turn round.'

Jason, taken by surprise at the sheriff's move, now lunged in an attempt to wrest the gun from him. 'No!' he shouted. 'That's not what we came fer.' For the first time he noticed that the silver star was missing from the sheriff's shirt.

Kelly avoided the clumsy attempt with a vicious sweep of his clenched fist that caught Jason on the side of the head and sent him reeling backwards. 'It's what I came fer,' he grated. 'I'm takin' him in. You stay outa this. Five thousand dollars will see me jest fine fer the rest of my life.'

Jason pushed himself off the wall, rubbing his head ruefully. 'I might've known you'd pull a stunt like this.' He took another quick step towards the sheriff and grabbed his arm.

The movement caused the sheriff's finger to tighten on the trigger of the small gun and its tiny bullet smacked into Adam's side.

The wound was not enough to disable the outlaw and he swung round, raising his Winchester in anger. At that very instant the crack of a rifle shot split the air and the lawman staggered backwards, clutching his chest. He took two faltering steps and sank, first to his knees, then to the ground and lay still.

Both the other men whirled, searching for the source of the shooter. In the same movement they threw themselves flat and rolled into whatever cover was nearest to them, Adam behind a water butt, Jason in the shelter of the wall.

A second shot followed closely on the first and dust kicked up into Jason's face. A third shot took Adam in the back.

From what Jason could judge the shots were coming from the top of the nearest bluff, to the left of the shack. 'Goddamn it! Who the hell's shooting at us now?' Both the sheriff and the outlaw had been deliberately targeted and he was sure he would be the next victim if he showed himself.

He called over to Adam who was cursing with the pain and trying to stem the flow of blood. 'Did Zeb follow you?'

'I must be gettin' careless.' There was an ominous rattle in his throat as he tried to form the words.

'You badly hurt?'

'Got me in the back. Cain't move.'

'That bad, huh. Can you hold out till I come back for you?'

'What're you plannin' to do?'

Jason stated the obvious. 'We're sitting ducks. If'n we don't do something he'll pick us off one at a time.' He lifted his head and raised his voice. 'I know it's you up there, Zeb. I'm gonna kill you. Should've done it long ago.'

Zeb's voice, full of venom, yelled back, 'You're all dead men. There's nowhere you kin go. Come an' get me if you can.'

Jason quickly assessed the situation.

Although he was unhurt he was unarmed and his horse and weapons were some fifty yards away. The sheriff was clearly dead and Adam was out of the reckoning. At the same time Zeb was somewhere near by and wanted to kill them both. Even if they waited until dark there was a danger that Zeb could lie in wait for them as they retrieved their horses. And there was a wounded man to consider.

Doing nothing was not an option.

'Can you throw me yer rifle?' he called to Adam, but immediately saw that it was lying in the open and that it was going to be impossible for either of them to reach it without being shot. 'What about yer six-gun? Kin you toss that over to me?'

'Yeah. You kin have that 'cos I sure ain't gonna need it where I'm heading.'

The Colt flew through the air and landed ten feet out of Jason's reach. It had hardly come to rest when a bullet from Zeb's rifle spurted dust just inches from it.

'Dang it,' Jason breathed, 'the varmint's playing with me.' He looked around for something to use to hook it towards him. He took off his vest and, holding it by a corner, threw it over Adam's gun. Zeb's rifle spoke again and another slug punched a hole in the material. The Colt was undamaged as Jason dragged it through the dirt.

'Gotcha!' he shouted in triumph.

'You goin' after him?' Adam's voice was barely above a whisper and Jason had to strain to hear it.

'Yep, I'm gonna nail the bastard.' He checked the chambers of the gun. 'Right,' he called. 'I'll be seein' yer.' He edged along the planking, keeping in the shelter of the wall. 'Stay where you are an' I'll be back. But first, I'll need yer hoss.'

'I ain't about to go nowhere,' Adam grated.

Without knowing exactly where the hidden marksman was concealed it was going to be difficult to gain the base of the escarpment twenty yards away.

Once there Jason would be protected, but he had to get there first.

He eyed Adam's palomino and made encouraging noises in the hope of enticing the animal to come to him. It took no notice except to look at him with inquisitive eyes.

'What do I have to say to your hoss to git it to obey?' he called.

There was an ominous silence, then, 'Click yer fingers an' say, 'C'mere',' Adam said. 'An' you need a firm hand.' This time Jason sensed the effort as Adam spoke.

He smiled ruefully and followed instructions. 'I should've tried that first,' he muttered as the horse pricked its ears and lifted its head, then ambled over to allow Jason to take hold of the reins.

'I hope Zeb's an animal lover,' he mumbled to himself as he gave the horse a slap on the rump and set it off, racing by its side, urging it on, so that the animal was between him and the shooter. Either he had taken Zeb by surprise or perhaps he was reloading, but there were no further shots and he reached the foot of the rocks without incident.

He mounted and felt the horse show its resentment at a strange rider. He spoke softly but held the reins tight, gripping hard with his knees, taking command. The horse responded and Jason urged it on, keeping close to the rock face, searching for an easy way up to the top of the butte.

What he found was a cleft in the sheer face, as if a giant had wielded an axe and split it in half. Further in the cleft opened out into a narrow canyon, snaking as it went further into the rock and cutting out much of the light from the sun.

Jason entered cautiously, conscious that he was probably riding into danger.

About thirty yards further on he found a scree-strewn slope leading upwards where the cliff face had fallen away. He urged the horse up. He emerged at the top on to a flat rocky area with almost no vegetation capable of concealing a man. But the surface was strewn with rocks of various sizes behind any of which Zeb could be waiting. He slid from the saddle and took shelter, sweeping his gaze around, trying to assess the possibilities of an ambush.

Yet not only was there no sight of his quarry, there was no sudden crack of the expected rifle shot, no noise to break the silence except for the breathing of his horse.

Suddenly he heard the clatter of hoofs on rock, a horse being ridden away from him, then the sound of a rifle being fired several times, the shots seemingly wild, posing no threat.

He briefly saw the fleeing figure of Zeb riding his horse at full gallop, before animal and rider disappeared. He understood then that Zeb was enjoying himself, playing a game of cat and mouse, wanting him to follow. And Zeb seemed confident that he would.

Zeb was right; he would play the

game and accept the challenge, although he recognized he was at a serious disadvantage having only a handgun against Zeb's rifle.

He leapt back on to the saddle and raced after his quarry across the hard surface, oblivious of the dangers. It seemed he was on a plateau with no way down until he noticed that, where there had been a further earth slide, the flat surface of the rock was split and another slope led down to the canyon, the floor of which was strewn with loose boulders.

It was down this that Zeb had ridden at reckless speed. Jason followed more cautiously and saw that Zeb was now some hundred yards ahead.

'Zeb,' he shouted, the steep walls echoing his words, 'I'm comin' for yer.'

'I'm waiting,' Zeb called back.

But where, for Zeb had disappeared? There was a range of options for which a shooter might lie in wait. The most likely, Jason thought, was where the canyon curved about thirty yards ahead and where a huge chunk of red rock had tumbled and come to rest, restricting the width of the canyon floor.

A man on horseback approaching the bend would make an easy target, to be picked off like a sitting bird. Jason reined in behind a shoulder of rock. Before considering his plan of attack he had to be sure where his enemy was.

'Give yersel' up, Zeb,' he shouted.

'You'll have to help me,' Zeb shouted back. 'My hoss threw me.'

Jason smiled grimly, so obvious was it that this was a ploy. But even if true Zeb would still be a dangerous man. 'If you're lookin' fer my help throw out yer weapons.'

To his surprise a rifle was laid on top of the boulder, followed by a .45 Colt.

'Quick.' Zeb's voice sounded weak. 'I'm bleedin' bad an' my leg's broke.'

'I'm comin' in slow,' Jason said, but he dug the spurs in hard and covered the short distance at top speed, crouching low over the gelding's neck.

He was not surprised when he saw Zeb spring to his feet, snatch the rifle and bring it up to point in his direction.

But he was too late. Jason set his horse to leap over the rocks while at the same time he threw himself from the saddle, his Colt in his hand, the hammer already pulled back.

He and Zeb went down in a tangle of arms and legs. The rifle discharged harmlessly but Jason's finger automatically jerked on the trigger, the bullet finding its mark in Zeb's heart. Zeb did not get up.

It was over so quickly that Jason hardly had time to think. Now he heaved himself off the inert body and filled his lungs with air.

Epilogue

Hal Skandy cleaned his hands on an ink-stained rag and patted the large iron printing press affectionately. He grinned broadly at Jason. 'This machine's bin working overtime since you came,' he said. 'You've bin in the news pert near every day.'

'Not my choice.' Jason shrugged.

'Shame about Marl.'

'Yeah. She didn't deserve that.'

'How many dead bodies have you brung in?'

Jason pretended to count on his fingers. 'Six.'

'Bounty on the heads of a couple o' those should be comin' your way.'

'Seems like it,' Jason agreed.

'We've seen the last of the Redford gang, I reckon. Should've bin seven bodies, though, shouldn't it?'

'Don't reckon.'

'Adam One-ear. What about him? Are you gonna come clean about what happened out there? Sizeable bounty on that varmint.'

'Yeah,' Jason said. 'Could've set a man up fer a long time.' The sheriff had thought so, too, and he had died.

Jason was satisfied. He had given the sheriff a good send-off and had paid his debt to Adam in the only way he could. 'I've already told my story,' he said.

Hal rubbed his ear. 'Not sure we've got to the truth. I could make up a tale but the *Inspiration Clarion*'s an honest paper.'

'The committee believed me. So you kin report everything I've said with a clear conscience. I ain't about to change a word.'

'You mean that Adam just rode out while the sheriff was savin' yer life?'

Jason met his gaze. 'Yep. That's about the size of it.'

'Kelly was a good man, fer sure,' Hal agreed.

He came to a decision. 'OK, this is

how it'll read. 'Kelly Quintock, sheriff of Inspiration for more'n many years, unlawfully killed in pursuance of his duty, was a brave and conscientious law officer. He will be sorely missed'. How does that sound?'

'Just dandy,' Jason said. 'Mebbe they'll put up a statue in his honour.'

'Which brings me to the next question,' Hal continued. 'I b'lieve you were front-runner to become our new sheriff. What made you turn it down? You could handle it an' the pay's not bad.'

Jason grinned and seemed to ponder the question. 'When I drifted into Inspiration,' he said, 'I hadn't more'n a few dollars to call my own an' only the clothes I stood up in. No plans. Nothin'. Then, within the space of a few days I was offered four jobs. A man can't expect better'n that.'

'Four jobs?'

'Yeah. First I got the offer o' workin' as a wrangler at the CB ranch. I was prepared to accept that. Then,' he threw

Hal a wicked grin, 'as an assistant to an ornery newspaper editor. Could've bin fun and I thought hard about it.

'Then, after that I was asked to be sheriff o' this town.'

Hal waited for him to go on. 'That's three. You said there was four.'

'Ah, yes,' Jason said, as if he had forgotten. 'The fourth? Well, I kinda put myself forward fer that one. Pay might not be as good an' seems there's a load o' graftin' involved. An' I'd have to smarten myself up.'

'Well?' Hal asked, intrigued.

Jason's grin was broad. 'The job means gettin' closely involved with the prettiest young lady this side o' the Rocky Mountains. An' probably the other side, too.'

'I see,' Hal said, his expression serious. 'And which job are you gonna take?'

Other titles in the
Linford Western Library:

KILL SLAUGHTER

Henry Remington

When a California train is robbed of $30,000, and two Pinkerton detectives are killed, bounty hunter James Slaughter rides to investigate. But a cloud of fear hangs over the railroad town of Visalia, and even the judge is running scared. Beaten up, jailed and framed by the sheriff's deputies, Slaughter survives assassination attempts — but is hit by still more trouble as a vicious range war erupts on the prairie . . .

LAWLESS GUNS

M. Duggan

Imprisoned for murder, innocent Luther Larkin feels only resentment towards the town of Black Bear Crossing and its lawman. When an unexpected confession sets Luther free, he finds himself drawn back to his boyhood home — and pretty soon trouble seeks him out. Nor is he the only one who has been drawn back to Black Bear Crossing: deranged killer Donald Ricket has a score to settle with the town, and only Luther stands between him and his goal . . .